THE TEMPLAR DETECTIVE AND THE LOST CHILDREN

A TEMPLAR DETECTIVE THRILLER

Also by J. Robert Kennedy

James Acton Thrillers

The Protocol
Brass Monkey
Broken Dove
The Templar's Relic
Flags of Sin
The Arab Fall
The Circle of Eight
The Venice Code
Pompeii's Ghosts
Amazon Burning
The Riddle
Blood Relics
Sins of the Titanic
Saint Peter's Soldiers
The Thirteenth Legion
Raging Sun
Wages of Sin
Wrath of the Gods
The Templar's Revenge
The Nazi's Engineer
Atlantis Lost
The Cylon Curse
The Viking Deception
Keepers of the Lost Ark
The Tomb of Genghis Khan
The Manila Deception
The Fourth Bible
Embassy of the Empire
Armageddon
No Good Deed

Special Agent Dylan Kane Thrillers

Rogue Operator
Containment Failure
Cold Warriors
Death to America
Black Widow
The Agenda
Retribution
State Sanctioned
Extraordinary Rendition
Red Eagle
The Messenger

Templar Detective Thrillers

The Templar Detective
The Parisian Adulteress
The Sergeant's Secret
The Code Breaker
The Black Scourge
The Unholy Exorcist
The Lost Children

Kriminalinspektor Wolfgang Vogel Mysteries

The Colonel's Wife
Sins of the Child

Delta Force Unleashed Thrillers

Payback
Kill Chain
Infidels
Forgotten
The Lazarus Moment
The Cuban Incident

Detective Shakespeare Mysteries

Depraved Difference
Tick Tock
The Redeemer

Zander Varga, Vampire Detective

The Turned

THE TEMPLAR DETECTIVE AND THE LOST CHILDREN

J. ROBERT KENNEDY

UNDERMILL PRESS

This is a work of fiction. Names, characters, places, and incidents are products of the author's imagination. Any resemblance to actual persons, living or dead, is entirely coincidental.

ISBN: 9781990418181

First Edition

The man who inspired and entertained us for decades,
and to whom this book is dedicated.
Who is Alex Trebek?

The Templar Detective and the Lost Children

A Templar Detective Thriller

"Concerning terra Salica, no portion or inheritance is for a woman, but all the land belongs to members of the male sex who are brothers."

As translated from Salic Civil Law Code, circa AD 500

"The best inheritance a father can leave his children is a good example."

John Walter Bratton

AUTHOR'S NOTE

This is the seventh novel in this series, and for those who have read the others and embraced these characters as so many of you have, please feel free to skip this note, as you will have already read it.

The word "detective" is believed to have originated in the mid-nineteenth century, however, that doesn't mean the concept of someone who investigated crime originated less than two hundred years ago. Crime long predated this era, and those who investigated it as well.

The following historical thriller is intended to be an entertaining read for all, with the concept of a "Templar Detective" a fun play on a modern term. The dialog is intentionally written in such a way that today's audiences can relate, as opposed to how people might have spoken in Medieval France, where, of course, they conversed in French and not English, with therefore completely different manners of speaking, and of addressing one another. For consistency, English phrasing is always used, such as Mister instead of Monsieur. This does not mean they will be speaking to each other as rappers and gangsters, but will instead communicate in ways that imply comfort and familiarity, as we would today. If you are expecting, "Thou dost hath offended me, my good sir," then prepareth thyself for disappointment. If, however, you are looking for a fast-paced adventure, with plenty of action, mystery, and humor, then you've come to the right place.

Enjoy.

PREFACE

In thirteenth-century France, as was true in most of Europe if not the world, women's rights of inheritance were limited. When her husband died, it was up to the heir of his title and fortune to take care of her, and if that weren't possible, then her own birth family.

This led to many difficult situations, especially for nobility, where titles and vast wealth were at stake. Where there are money and power, there are jealousies, more often than not petty. These petty jealousies could result in rivalries that continued past death. Should a nobleman die without a son, his fortune would transfer to the most senior male relative, usually a younger brother, uncle, or cousin.

But what if that relationship were estranged? Estranged to the point where one was certain the heir to one's title and fortune would leave one's wife and daughter destitute, as revenge for perceived affronts?

If faced with such an impossible situation, how far would you go to ensure your family's future should you be not long for this earth? Would you lie? Cheat? Would you sin?

And ultimately, would you murder if it meant your family had a secure future after you were gone?

Lord François de Montglat Estate
Paris, Kingdom of France
AD 1298

Lord François de Montglat cringed at yet another wail from the opposite side of the door he now paced in front of. Helene, his eldest daughter, sat in a chair across from the door, tears rolling down her cheeks as she wrung her hands with worry. His other four girls all wanted to be here to support their mother, however they were too young to hear such things, and he had sent them away after the first blood-curdling scream.

His wife Denise was too old for this. All of her births had been difficult, and the Court physician and every midwife involved over the years had told them they should give up. Yet they had no choice. They had five wonderful daughters that he adored, but none of that mattered. They were girls, and though he had no doubt they would grow up to be terrific women who would marry well and bear him countless grandchildren, this was France, and females had no right of inheritance.

He desperately needed a son, otherwise, when he died, his wife and children would lose everything.

By law, his brother would get the family fortune, and that couldn't be allowed to happen. He was a vile creature whom he hadn't spoken to in over a decade. Out of duty, he sent him a more than adequate monthly stipend that allowed him to enjoy a lifestyle far better than the vast majority ruled by the nobility he was fortunate enough to be born into. If he died tomorrow, and his brother chose to punish him in the afterlife, his wife and children could be destitute, and any future he had hoped his daughters might have, would be ended, for none of the senior ruling class would want to marry into an impoverished family.

His wife was nobility, of course, and normally her family would step in should the nightmarish scenario come true. Unfortunately, her family, while respected, was never wealthy, and as she was an only child, the family's assets were long gone to a distant cousin she hadn't seen since her parents died many years ago.

No one could help them.

Only a male heir.

Another wail had him pulling at his thinning hair. He had been on the other side of the door for every one of his daughters' births, and none had sounded like this. This had to end. They couldn't try for another child, otherwise he might lose his wife, and that was something he couldn't live with.

If she makes it through this, we need to try another way.

There was another way, and he had prepared for this. God had decided, for some reason, He would only give him girls, so he fully expected that if a child were born today, it would be a sixth daughter, not a first son. As well, the physician and midwife had warned him that the prospects of a healthy child were slim, and his wife had said she hadn't felt any movement for days.

He feared the worst.

Another scream, unlike any he had yet heard, one filled with anguish and pain, had him dropping to his knees, his hands clasped in front of his chin as he stared up at the heavens, tears filling his eyes as fear gripped his heart.

He was losing his wife.

"Oh, God, please get her through this! Please don't punish her for my sins!"

His daughter was immediately at his side, her arms wrapped around him tightly as she sobbed, and he regretted his decision to let her stay.

No child, no matter how old, should hear their mother die.

He held her tight as he finished his prayer, then whispered in her ear. "You should go."

She shook her head vehemently. "I want to stay with you."

He hugged her harder, then everything fell silent on the other side of the door and his chest ached at the implications. There was no crying baby, there was no joyous relief, there was no chatter among the servants assisting in the birth.

There was nothing but the echoing sobs of him and his daughter.

The door swung open and the lady's maid, Madeleine, stepped out. He quickly rose to his feet, wiping his eyes dry with the back of his hand, and stared at the woman he had known for years, and who had faithfully served his wife for almost as long as they had been married. She shook her head and his heart crawled up into his throat.

"My wife?"

"It's too early to tell."

"May I see her?"

She stepped aside. He pointed at the chair his daughter had been sitting in. "You stay here."

"But I want to see her."

"You will. But let me first."

His daughter acquiesced, returning to her chair, and François entered the room, more scared to step forward here than on any battlefield. The chambermaid, Charlotte, was in the corner with a bundle, a bundle silent and unmoving, and his wife lay on the bed, blood, sweat, and tears soaking her and the sheets. The midwife, Jaqueline, was cleaning her, but stepped aside as he entered, bowing. He dismissed her fealty with a wave, saying nothing as he took a knee beside his wife's bed and gripped her hand. She turned toward him, pale and exhausted, her long hair drenched.

"Forgive me, husband."

He forced a smile. "There is nothing to forgive. What happened here today was God's will and had nothing to do with you. For whatever reason, he has decided we shall never be blessed with a son." He kissed her hand. "I swear, I will never put you through that again."

She closed her eyes, tears flowing once again. "Then what shall we do?"

He leaned closer, whispering in her ear. "We'll do what we discussed."

She didn't open her eyes, but she nodded. "We have no choice, though what we are about to do sickens my heart."

"As it does mine, but we have no choice." He leaned in and kissed her forehead then rose, turning to the others. He pointed at the bundle of his stillborn child. "What was it?"

Charlotte turned to him. "Another daughter, milord."

He closed his eyes and sighed heavily. "Then it was

for nothing." He opened his eyes and squared his shoulders as he drew in a slow, deep breath, steeling for what was about to happen. He indicated the bundle that would have been his sixth daughter, then addressed their trusted lady's maid, Madeleine. "Treat her with the respect she deserves. Bury her in the family graveyard, however, do so discreetly. No marker."

"As you wish, milord."

He held up a finger. "I have one final instruction for you all."

His wife wept and his staff gasped as he delivered the message that had his own stomach churning.

Thibault Residence
Paris, Kingdom of France

Thomas Durant sat in the cubbyhole that was his office. The only true one was Mrs. Simone Thibault's, not ten paces from where he hovered over his desk. To those who didn't know his employer, she was a wretched woman, but in the months under her employ, he had come to know her as much more than the façade she presented to the public. She wasn't a good woman, though she wasn't heartless. She and her late husband had started a loansharking business years ago, and after he had passed, she had turned it into something much grander than he was capable of. Now she dabbled in far more than just loaning money at exorbitant rates of interest to the desperate souls of the slums of Paris. She had her fingers into everything. If somebody wanted something, she knew how to get it, and the poor and the rich alike would climb those stairs to her office and make their requests.

He both hated and loved what he did. He kept track of all her finances, the outstanding loans, the balances, the interest, who was overdue. It was all managed by him, and that was the part he loved—working with the numbers. His late father had been a forger, capable of incredible feats, hand-drawing documents that would fool even the King. Thomas had tried his hand at it, his father hoping to give him a vocation that would carry him through his adult years, but Thomas had failed miserably. He simply couldn't draw, couldn't forge the seals or the flourishes of a signature.

But he could read, he could write, and he could do all the math necessary to perform this task for Thibault, and if he ignored what the numbers represented, he sometimes didn't hate the work he did. Yet each line represented another person, another family that was desperate, but as she had explained to him, each line also represented an opportunity for that same person, for that same family. No one was lending money to people like this, except people like her. If it weren't for her, these people wouldn't be able to repair a home damaged by fire, take their child to a physician, repair the damaged oven in their bakery. If it weren't for people like her, the family that lived in that burned-down home would be homeless, the child who needed that physician would die, the baker whose oven needed to be repaired would go out of business.

And these people always agreed to the terms.

But they did so because they were desperate. Only the desperate came up those stairs, and far too many had no hope of ever repaying the debt. The best most could hope for was to keep paying the interest due, which made Thibault a very wealthy woman, but one who would never be welcomed into high society, though he had never heard her express any interest in doing so. She seemed content to live in the slums at a level far higher than those around her, though it made for a lonely life, he was sure. She attempted to hide it, but on occasion, when she didn't know he was looking, he had caught her staring out the window, an expression on her face that couldn't be described in any other way than desperately sad, desperately lonely. She had created a life that could have been quite pleasurable if she had someone to share it with, but he feared she would be alone until the day she died.

Perhaps that's why she had taken him in. He had lost his mother years ago, then his father had been murdered last year. When circumstance had brought them together, and she had discovered his skills, she had offered him a job, and out of desperation, he had taken it. He had no other prospects, for there was little to be had beyond manual labor in the slums, and he was shamefully weak.

Initially, he had dreaded coming here every day. Thibault's only companion, her enforcer and protector, Enzo, a hulking beast of a man whose mangled face would provide a lifetime of nightmares for any child, was terrifyingly intimidating, and Thomas walked on eggshells every moment he had been around the man. Though Enzo was terrifying in his own way, so was Thibault. Yet over these past months, Enzo had proven a better friend than any he had ever had, extending his protection duties to include him. Underneath his hardened exterior lay a heart as lonely as Thibault's, as desperate to find a family of any sort that could love him, and that he could love. He had found it here, and the two of them, now three, made for the oddest family in the slums.

Yet he had another family, a family that had welcomed him with open arms, a family far more appealing on a human level, and a family that now included the woman he loved, the only woman he had ever loved.

Isabelle.

He had met a group of Templars led by a knight named Sir Marcus de Rancourt that had become involved in the murder of his father. They had brought the murderer to justice and eventually embraced Thomas, always checking in on him when they were in Paris, always helping him when he needed it, and finally offering him a home on the farm they now tended, their lives as active Templars behind them, though not so far that danger never found them.

And it was through them that he had met Isabelle Leblanc. They had fallen in love and now planned to marry. Doing so would normally mean giving up everything he had ever known, but working on a farm had no appeal to him whatsoever, so a compromise had been reached. During the growing season, they would stay at the farm to help, but in the off-season, they would stay in Paris where he could continue to stimulate his mind through his work with Thibault, and maintain the house he had spent so many years in with his family. Everyone had agreed it was a good solution to his conundrum, and he looked forward to their marriage where they could put their plan into action.

"Where are you, my boy?"

Thomas flinched at Thibault's voice, and was startled to see her standing beside him. "What?"

"Where are you? I've been standing here and you haven't noticed."

He blushed as he leaned back. "I'm sorry. I guess I've just been distracted."

She reached over and folded closed his ledger. "Enzo and I are going for a walk. Join us."

If he could, he would have said no. He had too much work to do, but you didn't say no to Thibault when she asked you to do something. He reluctantly rose, though hoped he hid his feelings well, and followed Enzo and Thibault down the stairs and out into the daylight. To anyone who hadn't lived here for an extended period, to call this air fresh would be an insult to God, for he was certain He had never intended it to smell like this.

Thomas had never really noticed it until he had visited the farm and experienced proper fresh air for the first time in his life. It was joyous, something you could sit outside and simply breathe in all day and never tire of. When he had returned to the city after that first experience, it had been soul-crushing to realize what he had been suffering with all these years, what everyone here suffered through, the rot and decay going unnoticed. Yet now, as he gazed about the streets, the sources were impossible to miss.

How much better our lives would be if we merely cleaned up after ourselves.

He sighed, and it didn't go unnoticed by Thibault.

"What troubles you, my boy?"

He waved his hand at the street in front of them. "The filth we live in."

Thibault assessed the area for herself then grunted. "It is rather disgusting, is it not? Little can be done about it, however, when so many live in such a confined space. She eyed him. "Why does this trouble you now? You've grown up here most of your life. You should know no different."

"The farm, ma'am," boomed Enzo.

"Ah, the farm. This is true. For the first time in your life, you've had a taste of how things were meant to be, rather than what sinful men have created for themselves on God's green earth. A little slice of Eden."

Thomas agreed. "Yes, ma'am."

"Perhaps when you are married and settled into your own home, you shall permit me a visit so I too can experience the joys of country life."

"It will be our pleasure, ma'am." His response didn't surprise him as he had no other choice than to at least pretend to be agreeable to her idea. What did surprise him was that he actually would be agreeable to her visiting, though he wondered if Isabelle would be.

She apparently picked up on his doubts, patting his arm and smirking. "Don't worry, my boy. The chances of me leaving all this"—she swept her arm—"is next to nothing."

He smiled slightly. "We would genuinely enjoy your company, ma'am. You've been so good to both Isabelle and me that hosting you would be our privilege."

She squeezed his arm and he caught her eyes glistening before she jerked her head away lest she show any emotion in public beyond anger. The people they walked among had to fear her, had to realize there were consequences to not paying her back. And he hated to admit it, but the surge of power he experienced when he and Enzo would walk through the streets, the crowds parting before them, was intoxicating. He had never cut an imposing figure, always slight of frame, barely a noticeable muscle on his body. It had always been his brain that got him through life, but walking through the streets with Enzo at his side to collect on overdue debts, the crowd scattering out of their way? It was fun to walk slightly ahead and imagine the enforcer wasn't with him, and that it was his own imposing figure that caused the fear among those who had often teased and derided him in his youth.

A man walked up to them, dressed as dapper as any

of the gentry that might be found slumming. His name was Hermant Passe, scum if there ever was one, the type of man Thomas had learned in his brief association with Thibault that he was lucky to have not fallen in with, for this man had no boundaries. When a debt was overdue with Thibault, Enzo was sent in to intimidate, sometimes to rough up, but far too often, Passe's delinquent debtors wound up dead, staked to a pole as a message to anyone else who dared not pay what was due.

Where Enzo might deliver a gut punch to someone, Passe's men would leave them a bloody pulp. Passe relished in the violence of the game he played, unlike Thibault, whom Thomas had learned tolerated it as a necessity sometimes, though never something to be enjoyed. And Enzo played his part. At first, Thomas had thought Enzo enjoyed the violence, but he had come to learn he didn't. It was merely a necessary evil, and unfortunately, one of the few talents he had that had allowed him to survive on the streets for years.

Thibault stopped, and Passe tipped his hat to her. "A lovely day, is it not?"

Thibault eyed him. "It was."

Passe chuckled. "I believe it still is. And if I've spoiled it for you, I apologize. When I spotted you, I simply had to come and thank you for your referral."

Her eyes narrowed. "Referral?"

"Yes, the gentleman you sent me last—"

She held up a hand, cutting him off. "I sent you no one last week nor ever. In my rage at what was asked of me, I may have spat out your name as the only person I could think of who would do something so vile, and your contented smile darkens my heart to think that I was right and you would indeed commit something so vile. There are lines that must be drawn even in our business, and apparently, your line is far darker than mine."

Passe's smile broadened and he shrugged. "Perhaps, however, my side of the line is far more lucrative than yours."

"And the fires that burn in your particular pit of Hell will be far hotter."

He shrugged again. "That very well may be, however, it's only a matter of degrees. I have little doubt the slab of stone reserved for you to be chained to for eternity will be just as unbearable."

Thomas gulped as Enzo's fists clenched.

Thibault took a step closer to Passe. "Never compare what I do to what you do. I provide a service that while some may see as vile, I see as a service nonetheless, and on my day of judgment, though the Lord might not agree with everything I've done, in the end, I'm confident He'll forgive me for any transgressions. But for you, if you've done what I think you've done, there can be no forgiveness. Eternal damnation is what you face, and should I be there alongside you, I'll at least take comfort in knowing that you'll suffer for eternity as well." She took a step back. "Now, I shall take my leave of you and enjoy the rest of this fine day the good Lord has provided us."

Passe tipped his hat, his smile gone, his lips pressed tightly together. "Good day." He gave the imposing Enzo a wide berth, and Thibault resumed her walk. Thomas scrambled to catch up, Enzo merely taking a few extra strides.

"Ma'am, what was that all about?"

She sighed, shaking her head slowly at him. "It's nothing that a young mind like yours should be troubled with. It would haunt you for the rest of your days to know what men are capable of when desperate."

Lambert Residence
Paris, Kingdom of France

Lambert woke with a start, bolting upright in bed. His wife stirred beside him. "What is it?"

"I thought I heard something." He cocked an ear, struggling to hear what had wakened him, finding nothing but the creaking of the house, a blustery wind blowing outside shaking the old timbers that held their humble home together. "I guess it was just the wind."

"Go back to sleep. God knows with the newborn we don't get enough of it as it is. We shouldn't be sacrificing it to nature's untimely tempest."

He smiled at her and lay back down, closing his eyes. They had been married only a year, and already his beautiful wife had born him a perfectly healthy son. Neither of them had done this before, though both had mothers willing to provide non-stop advice. His had said to never let the baby sleep in the same room as them, and hers had said to ignore the baby's crying otherwise he'd learn that if he wanted attention, all he had to do was make a fuss and one of his parents would come running.

All rules were ignored the first week, the crib his father had handcrafted sitting at the foot of the bed, every sound investigated by one of them, usually his wife. But after neither of them got any sleep, and the advice had been reiterated by his mother that the crib should be outside of their bedroom so that at least one of them could get some sleep, they had acquiesced, the crib now on the other side of the door, still close enough that they could hear anything. His mother-in-law's advice to ignore the baby still hadn't been heeded, though now one of them would creep to the door and listen to see if there were anything to truly be concerned with, and unfortunately, the majority of the times, they still investigated in person, though at least now one of them was getting sleep.

He drifted when a floorboard creaked. "*That* wasn't the wind." He flung his bedding aside and swung out of bed, his wife doing the same. "You heard that?"

"Yes," she whispered.

Another creak.

He grabbed a wooden club he kept under the bed just for an occasion such as this, though he had never had opportunity to use it. He gripped it tightly, wishing he had instead kept a dagger. He tiptoed to the door, cringing each time the boards betrayed him. He held out a hand in the dark, blocking his wife's path. "Lock the door behind me." He lifted the bar, the last line of defense against intruders, and opened the door. He peered into the darkness, the only light from slivers of the moon's glow piercing through gaps in the wooden walls revealing little. He stepped over to the crib but heard nothing. He reached in and cried out. "The baby's gone!"

His wife screamed. The bar to the bedroom chambers rattled as she tossed it aside and the door swung open. Hinges creaked at the front of the house and he bolted down the hallway, his wife on his heels. He spotted the door open, the shaft of moonlight illuminating their living area, a man silhouetted in the frame.

"Halt!" he shouted, continuing forward, but the

man ignored him. His son cried out as he woke from the shouting, his wail piercing the silence of the sleeping Parisian slum. The silhouette disappeared to the left with their son, and as he reached the door, another replaced it, a dagger glinting in front of him before it plunged into his stomach then twisted. He cried out in agony as he dropped his club, his hands reaching for the blade buried to the hilt, but his assailant had already withdrawn it, shoving him unceremoniously back inside. He collapsed on the floor, his warm blood pulsing through his fingers. His wife screamed, the blood-curdling terror abruptly cut off as her throat was slit and she crumpled to the floor.

Footfalls echoed then the door shut, the wails of their child slowly fading in the distance. He dragged himself over to his wife, little strength left when he finally reached her. "My love." His voice was barely a whisper, but it was the best he could manage. There was no response, and he could hear no breathing. Tears filled his eyes, the heartache in his chest overwhelming the agony in his stomach. He reached out to hold her, but the best he could manage was to drape his arm over her still body. Tears rolled down his cheeks as he prayed for his baby boy.

"Lord, please let no harm come to my son from those who have taken him." He gasped, his voice cracking, his strength failing him. "You are his father now."

Outside Paris, Kingdom of France

Hermant Passe stood by the side of the road, stomping his feet to stimulate his circulation. It was well past nightfall, the air damp with a chill to it that had him shivering. He pulled a flask from his pocket and unscrewed the cap, taking a swig before returning it to its discreet hiding place. Three of his men were with him, plus one of the ladies of ill repute he employed, holding the newly acquired baby he was being paid handsomely for.

He had done this before, and he had no doubt would do it again. The poor never sought babies—the poor could make their own. And the poor never had concerns over inheritance, for they had nothing to pass on after their deaths, and no one would come looking for what little they had. But the rich, they had plenty at risk without a male heir. Anything they might possess could be handed over to some distant relative who had no concerns for the women left behind. It made desperate men do desperate things, like his client tonight.

Who was late.

That, and the fact the baby hadn't stopped wailing for the past quarter-hour, had him annoyed.

"Would you shut that thing up?"

Giselle gave him a look. "What would you have me do, breastfeed it?"

He shrugged. "If you think it would help."

"I'm not lactating, you ignorant fool."

He clenched a fist and shook it at her. "Watch your tongue, woman."

Giselle blanched with fear. "I'm sorry, sir. It's just that this thing is driving me insane as well."

"Why don't you stick your finger in its mouth?" suggested one of his men, Bertaut.

Giselle did just that, and the baby immediately quieted.

Passe sighed. "Thank the good Lord for that." Grunts of agreement echoed from the group. "Correct me if I'm wrong, but did we not agree to meet at midnight?"

"That's what I heard, boss," said Bertaut.

"Maybe he can't tell time without a servant," suggested Giselle.

Passe chuckled. "Perhaps I charged him too much and he can no longer afford any." He held up a finger, cocking an ear to the night. "Someone's coming."

His men readied themselves, their hands on the hilts of their swords. Two lights approached, swaying from side to side, and he soon picked out a carriage with two horses, the coachman pulling up on the reins as he spotted them. Passe stepped forward, beckoning Giselle to join him as the door to the carriage opened and their client stepped out.

"You're late."

The fear and uncertainty in the man's eyes let Passe know he was in control of the situation, not his well-heeled client.

"We had, shall we say, difficulties, but we're here now." The baby made a sound and the man's eyes widened. "Is that him?"

"Yes, of course it is. Why the hell else would I be out here at this hour with a baby?"

"Of course, of course. May I see him?"

"You may inspect the goods, yes."

The man stepped over and Giselle held up the baby, bouncing him gently.

"And he's a boy?"

Giselle reached down and moved the cloth aside, removing any doubt.

"May I hold him?"

Passe shook his head. "Not until I see the other half of my payment."

"Of course, of course." The man leaned inside the carriage then handed over a healthy-sized purse. Passe took it, loosening the string at the top, eagerly counting out the gold coins. This was the part of the job he loved—the payment and the counting, each delicious clink of a coin against another signaling his increased wealth. This was what it was all about. Wealth. From wealth came power, and from power came respect. And depending on how he wielded that power and respect, fear could come with it.

And that was what he wanted.

He was born in the slums and had clawed his way to where he was today. He had enough accumulated to make sure his home was in good repair, his clothes were the finest outside of the nobility, and his belly was always full, usually a little too full. He had wine and women, though he would give it all up so long as he could keep the fear he saw in men's eyes when he entered a room. It was intoxicating, and he would fight tooth and nail before he'd ever give it up.

And the amount he had just earned from this job

would allow him to take on a couple more henchmen that would follow him around, intimidating any who didn't dare show that fear he demanded. Life was good because he showed no mercy, had no limits, and there were no lines he wasn't willing to cross.

He finished counting the coins, payment for a line Thibault wasn't willing to even approach, then returned them to the pouch, nodding at Giselle. "Well, girl, what are you waiting for? Give the man his son."

Giselle handed the small bundle over.

The man held the child then stared at Passe, his eyes glistening, his smile broad. "Thank you. You don't know how much this means to us."

"A pleasure doing business with you. Should you ever need anything else, you know how to reach me."

The man hesitated. "And his parents? They were well compensated?"

Passe smirked. "They won't be complaining, I can assure you."

This satisfied the man, and he climbed into the carriage then closed the door. The carriage pulled away and one of his men brought the horses over. Passe mounted his then hauled Giselle up behind him, intending to work off some steam with her when they returned home. He pointed at Bertaut.

"Find out where he goes. A man like that wants a male newborn for only one reason, and it might prove useful to have something we can use against a person like that should we run into trouble in the future."

"Yes, boss." Bertaut turned his horse around then took off after the carriage.

Passe headed them back toward the city, looking forward to the evening ahead.

"Can I hold it?"

He chuckled. "There'll be plenty of time for that when we get home."

Giselle giggled. "No, I mean the money. I've never seen so much money before in my life."

He fished the pouch out of his pocket and held it up. She eagerly snatched it and within moments, coins clanged together behind him. He glanced over his shoulder. "Don't forget, I know exactly how many are in there, so don't get any ideas."

There was a harrumph of disappointment. "You don't trust me?"

"Of course I don't trust you. You're surprised?"

"I guess not." She handed back the pouch and he returned it to his pocket, making a mental note to check the count when he got home. She leaned her head against his back, wrapping her arms around his waist, and he smiled as her hands did things no reputable woman would.

Life was good.

And he would slice the throat of any who would try to take it away.

Lord François de Montglat Country Estate
Outside St. Denis, Kingdom of France

It had been far too easy, and that was what was most disturbing about it. As Lord François de Montglat stared at his wife hugging their new son, his heart ached with what he had done. For now, Denise appeared unconcerned with the sin they had committed, this necessary evil required to save his family from destitution. Only he and his wife and those who had been in the room that night were aware of what had truly happened. As far as the rest of the household was concerned, a healthy baby boy had been born that night, then they had gone on a trip to their country estate to recover.

Though nothing could be further from the truth.

His stomach churned. The idea had never been his, had never been his wife's. It had been Sir John de Beaumont's. John had been in a similar situation a couple of years back, with three daughters and a serious illness he feared would take him before he'd ever have a chance to sire a male heir. Then one day, he introduced the King's Court to his newborn son. No one had even been aware his wife was pregnant, though most admitted to having not seen her in months. He had claimed a difficult pregnancy that required uninterrupted bed rest.

Unfamiliar with such things, François didn't question the story, having no reason to doubt his friend he had known for over a decade. It was over a little food and too much drink when the truth had been revealed after lamenting his own lack of a male heir, and his fears of what would become of his wife and daughters should he pass. John had confessed something so stunning, so shocking, François had refused to believe it and dismissed his friend's story as merely that, a story, concocted by a brain twisted with alcohol and the fear of impending death.

Yet the story had planted a seed, a seed that germinated more each day before its vile foliage spewed forth as the birth approached. He had no choice. He had to save his family, yet he hadn't known how, as John had succumbed to consumption several months ago. That had led him to the most scandalous member of the King's Court he could think of. Sir Denys de Montfort. If there were someone who knew how to get what he so desperately needed, what his family so desperately needed, it was Sir Denys, yet he couldn't trust the man with the truth. Instead, he had gone to Denys' home to merely get the name of someone who might help him attain something of a questionable nature. He had received a lecture on the dangers of opium, and Denys' emphatic pleas had proved a useful distraction, but he had eventually received a name after he had assured the man it had nothing to do with opium.

Mrs. Simone Thibault.

He had been in the slums of Paris on several occasions out of necessity. The filth, the vermin, the desperate poverty always made him uncomfortable, though nothing had prepared him for dealing with the criminal element. They were vile beyond compare, and delighted to be dealing with him. They would never know who he was, though there was no hiding what strata of society he belonged to. He had made certain he wore nothing that could identify him or his position, and that his carriage was stripped of all identifying marks. As far as the denizens of the slums would be concerned, he was a wealthy man, completely anonymous.

Thibault had rejected him, though a name she had mentioned in her tirade had led him to someone willing to help him. A deal was struck, and when his sixth daughter had died, he contacted the man to go ahead with the plan, and disturbingly quickly, a healthy newborn boy was delivered.

And it sickened him.

Yet it had also saved his family from a lifetime of horrors, and no one could deny that this boy, ignorant to his true origins, would enjoy a life far better than his parents could have ever given him, for this boy was now nobility, and would want for nothing.

He stepped over and brushed his hand over his son's thin hair.

Denise looked up at him. "He's beautiful, isn't he?"

He smiled. "He's everything we could have hoped for."

His wife gently kissed the boy's forehead. "We are your parents now, and we'll give you a life you could never have imagined."

François' mouth filled with bile and he excused himself, stepping out into the hallway and closing the door behind him. He leaned against the wall, sweat soaking his body. He drew a deep breath and headed for his office, swearing that every member of his staff whose path he crossed was staring at him, judging him for what he had done despite the fact only three should know.

Another thought crossed his mind. If the truth were revealed, he would be tossed in prison, the boy would be taken, and his family would lose everything, leaving them in the same position he was attempting to save them from. Only three knew his secret, three servants, three people of little consequence in this world.

He sat behind his desk and leaned forward, gripping his skull, squeezing hard then pulling at his hair, horrified at the thoughts consuming him. Yet were the crimes he now contemplated any worse than what he had already committed? He groaned in frustration. He could see no way around what must be done.

And as he justified these fresh horrors, any doubts as to where he would spend eternity were wiped away.

Outside St. Denis, Kingdom of France

It had become apparent quite quickly that the carriage belonging to his boss' client wasn't heading back into the city. It had taken several hours in the dark to reach its final destination, which in the dim moonlight appeared to be a country estate. A coat of arms was on the gates that Bertaut didn't recognize, though he couldn't honestly say he would even recognize the King's. These were simply things that didn't concern him. Nobility lived on the other side of the river in their fancy homes with their servants. His kind didn't mix with them, and never would, unless something nefarious was afoot like what had happened tonight.

Unfortunately, simply knowing where this estate was wouldn't fulfill his task. The boss wanted to know who this man was, yet he couldn't simply knock on the gate and ask the question. He would find out who lived here some other way, and that wouldn't be by asking the gentry that called the luxurious residences in this area their second home. No, the best people to ask were the laborers, and they wouldn't make an appearance until sunrise.

Unfortunately, he had expected to be following the carriage back into Paris, so was woefully unprepared for this journey. He had guided his horse well away from the home, then removed the beast's saddle, cleared a space to sleep, and built a small fire to provide him some semblance of warmth in the chilly night.

But now it was dawn, and those that provided for the comforts of the nobles that lived here were trudging along, executing their early morning duties, including deliveries. He repositioned just down the road from the residence in question and flagged down a farmer as he pulled out from the neighboring estate.

"Excuse me, sir. Could you tell me who lives in the next estate over?"

The farmer's eyes narrowed as he regarded him. "And why would I tell you such a thing?"

He suppressed his anger, instead shaking his head and rolling his eyes. "Because I'm a fool. My master gave me a message to deliver there, and told me to put it into the gentleman's hand. But for the life of me, I can't remember what the name was. If I go in there without knowing who I'm supposed to deliver the message to by name, it will shame my master."

The farmer's head slowly bobbed as he chuckled. "Yes, they are rather concerned about what people think of them, aren't they?" He pointed at the estate just down the road. "In this case, the man you're looking for is Lord François de Montglat. Very wealthy, very important. It's best you remember that name, for I'm certain your master wouldn't want to offend a man of his stature."

"Of course. Lord François de Montglat." He tapped his temple. "I'll remember that. Thank you so much for your help."

"It's my pleasure. Good day to you."

The farmer flicked the reins and his horse neighed, the heavy carriage laden with root vegetables pulling away and heading in the opposite direction of Lord François' estate. Bertaut headed toward the gates in case the farmer looked back, then as soon as he was out of sight, waited. Once he was satisfied enough time had passed that it might be believable the message had been delivered, he turned around and headed back toward Paris. He spotted the farmer ahead, rolling through the gates of the next estate. Bertaut slowed up to let him get through, then casually rode past, the farmer taking no notice.

Bertaut set out at a canter. It would take him hours to reach Paris, and he was long overdue from when the boss had expected him, but he had the information they needed, and all would be forgiven, as long as he could remember the name.

He cursed himself, finally seeing why knowing how to read and write could actually be useful. Instead of being able to write it down, he was forced to repeat the name over and over. He feared that by the time he reached Paris, he might have jumbled the words and invented an entirely new name.

And Passe would gut him for it.

Passe Residence
Paris, Kingdom of France

Passe sat behind his ornate desk, one of his prized possessions, handcrafted by a skilled artisan, designed to impress and intimidate. It was higher than normal, sitting atop a platform that extended beyond the footprint where his chair sat, a full foot higher than the floor. It meant he stared down on anyone who sat in his office, and it had always proven quite effective. His home was nothing like those enjoyed by the upper class, but in the slums, it might as well have been a palace. It was in exceptional condition compared to his neighbors, and his office and bed chambers, he was willing to bet, rivaled those of some of his most noteworthy of clients. They were the two rooms he spent the most time in—one conducting business, the other enjoying the company of one of his ladies then blissful sleep.

He always made certain that the journey from the door at street level and up the stairs to his office was as impressive as he could make it, not for the urchins that called the slums home, but for the men like Lord François, who now sat before him. They were out of their element, and made perhaps a little more comfortable with their situation when surrounded by some semblance of the wealth they were accustomed to.

He had been ready to gut Bertaut when he hadn't returned with his client's identity. He had assumed the fool had failed and was too scared to come back. But when he finally had, half a day late, the smile the name brought had been difficult to rid himself of, for Lord François de Montglat was a name he knew, and knew well. He made it his business to know the members of the King's Court and what their responsibilities were. He had done favors for several over the years, favors they wouldn't want made public. And it meant he owned them.

Like he owned this man.

And here he was, already sitting in his office for some unknown reason. He motioned at Bertaut who left the room and closed the door behind him.

"I must admit I'm surprised to see you again so soon. I trust there isn't a problem with the child?"

François' brightened slightly at the mention of his new son. "No, the boy isn't the problem, though I suppose he is."

Passe's eyes narrowed. "I'm not sure I understand."

"Three people are aware of the truth." François hesitated. "I can't risk my family's future over their ability to keep the secret."

Passe leaned back, folding his arms. "Yes, secrets have a habit of being revealed, and yours is a secret that must be kept for a lifetime. I see your problem."

François stared up at him. "Can you propose a solution?"

Passe smiled slightly. "We both know you didn't come here for me to propose a solution. You came here for me to enact one."

François' shoulders slumped as he sighed heavily. "You're right, of course, but I can't bring myself to say the words. When I began this undertaking, I was focused solely on acquiring the child. It never occurred to me what implications lay beyond that."

"Yet here we are. Who are these three people that know your secret?"

"Servants. A midwife, lady's maid, and chambermaid."

"Aren't you forgetting someone?"

François' eyes narrowed. "I don't believe so."

"The coachman who was there when you took delivery of the goods."

François' gasped. "I had forgotten!"

"That's why I'm here. Now, do they have families?"

"I'm—I'm sure they do."

"So, there are people that will miss them, that will ask questions."

"Yes, I suppose."

"So then, they can't just disappear."

"No, I suppose they can't."

"Then something has to happen to them that can't be tied back to you, that will leave their bodies to be found with the assumption being that they were killed in some innocent way for just being in the wrong place at the wrong time."

François stared at the floor, his voice low. "Yes, I suppose so." He glanced up. "Is this something you've done before?"

"Yes."

"So, you can help me?"

"I can, but it will cost you."

"How much?"

"Twice as much as for the child."

François' eyes shot wide. "That much?"

A smile spread across Passe's face. "Each."

François paled slightly then snapped out a curt nod. "Very well."

"Where are they now?"

"They're at my country estate with my wife and the baby."

"Good. Is there anyone they could have told?"

"I swore them to secrecy, and I'm confident they've kept everything to themselves for the moment. It's time that I fear will loosen their tongues."

Passe agreed. "Very well. I have an idea how we can resolve this swiftly. Return here tomorrow with the payment, and I'll give you my plan."

Lord François de Montglat Country Estate
Outside St. Denis, Kingdom of France

Madeleine climbed into the back of the carriage with the chambermaid Charlotte and the midwife Jaqueline, uncertain as to why they were being sent back to Paris without Lady Denise. As the lady's maid, she couldn't recall the last time they had been apart. She could understand the others being sent ahead to prepare for the Lady and the child's arrival at their home in Paris, but with everything going on, she was on edge.

The child had been stillborn.

She had buried her on the grounds that very night, then the Lord and Lady had gone to the country estate under the guise of recuperating from the birth, though the secret of its unsuccessful nature hadn't been revealed to anyone, including the daughters, though she was certain the eldest knew.

And then a baby had appeared, a healthy baby boy, a newborn declared as their son and male heir. Needless to say, she had been stunned. They all had been, though no one dared say anything. A baby girl had been born and had been dead before the contractions had even begun. A second baby hadn't been born later as was claimed by Lady Denise. She had been with the Lady the entire night. This was not a twin to the stillborn child.

This was someone else's baby.

Yet he was to be treated as if he were legitimately theirs.

It was troubling, to say the least. Where had this

baby come from? Whose was it? She wasn't a fool. She was well aware that her masters were desperate for a male child, as only a male could inherit in today's France, and with relations with the master's brother poor at best, he couldn't be relied upon to care for the Lady or their five daughters.

The dead child was their last hope, and that poor creature, returned to God's hands, had been a girl regardless. It was clear to her that in their desperation, they had acquired a child, but from where? Who would willingly give up a newborn? She supposed there were many, if she thought about it. There were orphanages, though orphanages asked questions, and if the secret got out, the child's lineage would be challenged. The scandal would not only destroy the Lord's reputation, it would seal the fate of those he was trying to save from his brother, for once the wretch found out his own sibling had attempted to cut him out of his rightful inheritance, it would guarantee a life of misery for the Lady and her daughters.

No, something like this had to be done quietly, anonymously.

She shivered as the carriage got underway.

"What is it?" asked Jaqueline.

"Nothing."

"You know something, don't you?"

Madeleine eyed her. "What do you mean?"

Jaqueline leaned forward, lowering her voice in case the coachman could hear. "You know where that baby came from."

Madeleine vehemently shook her head. "I have no idea."

Charlotte grunted, folding her arms as she leaned

back. "Well, we all know where he *didn't* come from, now don't we?"

Jaqueline turned to her. "What do you mean?

"Well, he certainly didn't come from her ladyship's cursed womb."

Jaqueline's head bobbed. "They must have gotten him from an orphanage. God knows there are plenty of children who could use a good home. I really feel for them. It's simply not fair. The Lady comes from nobility. Why should she and her children suffer when the patriarch dies just because they're women?"

Madeleine sighed. "It's always been that way and it always will be. But is that any excuse to take a baby?"

Two sets of eyes shot wide. "Take?" exclaimed Jaqueline.

Madeleine admonished her outburst with a glare.

Jaqueline paled, leaning in closer. "What do you mean, 'take?' Do you mean steal?"

"I don't know. They certainly didn't go to an orphanage. Too many questions would be asked. And if word got out that the boy wasn't theirs by blood, the scandal would destroy the family and defeat the purpose of acquiring the child."

"Then whose is it?"

Madeleine shrugged. "They must have arranged it with someone they knew. They could have paid someone to give up their child."

Charlotte's eyes narrowed. "But wouldn't that mean there'd be someone out there who knew their secret? That's a secret that needs to be kept forever. Can you really trust anyone forever? People change. People become desperate. I don't know if I'd want my entire family's future resting upon whether someone could hold their tongue for the rest of their lives."

Jaqueline scratched behind her ear, a puzzled expression on her face. "It doesn't make sense though. The timing would have to be perfect, and certainly would have to be arranged ahead of time. I suppose they could have planned on the baby being born a girl or stillborn, but that boy was a newborn, at most a week or two old. Could they time a birth so perfectly?"

Madeleine's stomach churned as she slowly shook her head. "No, you're right. They couldn't."

"Then what does that mean?"

Madeleine's heart raced, for it could mean only one thing. The baby had been taken from someone suddenly. The question was, had that person been compensated and the baby given up willingly, or was the baby kidnapped, taken against the parents' will? Either way, the family she served was cursed. The male heir to the family fortune and name was illegitimate, and perhaps the victim of a crime. Whatever the source of the child was, legitimate or otherwise, he wasn't blood, and if the secret came out, there would be hell to pay. A wave of weakness swept over her as a thought crossed her mind. "We know the secret," she murmured.

Her two companions stared at her. "What do you mean?" asked Jaqueline.

"The three of us. We're the only ones who know the secret."

"So?"

"So? Do you think the Lord and Lady trust us enough with their futures?"

Jaqueline stared at her, her head tilted slightly to the side. "What are you getting at?"

"What I mean is, if you were nobility, and all of that could be taken away if one terrible secret were revealed, and I, nobody of importance, was the only one who knew your secret, would you let me live?"

De Rancourt Family Farm
Crécy-la-Chapelle, Kingdom of France

Sir Marcus de Rancourt stood and stretched his back then rotated his shoulder, wounded in his last official battle in the Holy Lands. While recovering, he had received a letter from his sister giving him the horrifying news that she was dying, and that there was no one left to care for his niece and nephew. He had never been there for his family, having left as a teenager to join the holy order. His family was nobility, though of the sort that true nobility sneered at. He had no wealth, only his name, but that had been enough for the Poor Fellow-Soldiers of Christ and of the Temple of Solomon.

The Knights Templar.

They had embraced him as a knight, and the over two decades in that holy order had made him the man he was today. And he hadn't regretted a moment of it until he had received that letter. With his shoulder injured, he was of no use defending the pilgrims he was sworn to protect, so he had returned home to see what could be done about the children. His trusted sergeant and squires had insisted on accompanying him, and he was glad for it.

His sergeant, Simon Chastain, was the best friend he had ever known, though in the eyes of those who concern themselves with station, they shouldn't have such a familiarity. Those things were of no importance to him. He was no better than any other man simply because he was born with a name and a bloodline that favored him over others. Yes, while on duty, his sergeant was his sergeant, his squires were his squires, and though they all did his bidding, he always treated them with respect, and the loyalty that resulted went far beyond anything fear and degradation could provide.

And that had been proven when he remained in France to raise his young niece and nephew rather than see them handed over to the church. The loyalty shown by Simon and his squires, David and Jeremy, when they had insisted on staying with him and building a new life together, had warmed his heart, as if the good Lord himself had reached down from the heavens and blessed him personally.

His life had changed entirely in this past year, and though his decision had been reluctant, this family that he had rediscovered, the family expanding with new members they had taken in over the past months, was more rewarding than anything he had experienced in the Holy Lands.

Isabelle and Thomas would soon be married, and they intended to live and work this farm during the growing season. Lady Joanne de Rohan and her former chambermaid, Beatrice, had settled into the farmhouse as refugees from a system that punished women for being women after their husbands died. And young Pierre Fabron, orphaned the week they had arrived, now was like a brother to Marcus' niece and nephew.

"My God, what did you eat?" cried Jeremy.

Marcus grinned at the outburst from the barn.

Then there were the animals. They had quite the family here, from humans to farm animals to the farm's mastiff, Tanya, desperate for a new master, and eagerly finding one in Marcus. The dog was rarely out of sight and was extremely protective, not to mention useful in a fight. Her sheer size would fill a man's heart with terror if he saw the snarling beast sailing through the air toward him, and at times, Marcus thanked the good Lord the beast was on his side.

Jeremy stepped out of the barn. "All right, who's the joker?"

Marcus eyed him. "What are you talking about?"

"Every one of the cows has diarrhea. They were perfectly healthy yesterday, and now the whole floor of this barn is swimming in shit. How in all that is holy am I supposed to clean it?"

"Carefully?" suggested Simon.

Jeremy gave Simon the stink-eye. "Useful suggestions would be appreciated."

Simon roared with laughter. "Am I ever glad I'm no longer a squire! My shit-shoveling days are over."

Marcus gave his old friend a look. "Rank may have its privileges, but on a farm, everyone pitches in."

Simon's eyes shot wide. "You're not serious, are you? You really expect me to shovel cow diarrhea?"

"Somebody has to do it."

Simon jabbed a finger at each of the two squires. "Yes, and there are your two somebodies."

Jeremy grinned. "We really could use as many hands as possible."

Simon glared at him. "You'll keep your mouth shut if you know what's good for you."

"No can do. I'm too busy breathing through my mouth. If I breathe through my nose, I'm liable to vomit."

Marcus headed for the barn and his eyes watered at

the unusually fierce stench, his youngest squire, who was by no means young, not exaggerating. "Are the cows ill?"

Jeremy shrugged. "What do I know of cows? I have to assume something's wrong since they've all blasted the barn with a healthy dosing of what I would characterize as a shit storm."

Marcus stepped inside. He gagged at the overwhelming stench, memories of latrines in the desert heat not helping. He held a hand over his mouth and nose, struggling to take shallow breaths to no avail.

"You see what I'm dealing with? How am I supposed to clean this up?"

"Just cover it with hay."

Everyone spun to see Marcus' nephew, Jacques, standing in the entrance.

"What's that, Nephew?" asked Marcus.

"Cover it with hay. It will soak it up then you just shovel out the hay. You'll get most of it."

Marcus thought about it for a moment. The idea was simple yet brilliant. "Where did you get the idea, my boy?"

"Father did it once when the cows got sick." His eyes glassed over at the mention of his late father who had died saving his younger sister from drowning.

David took a knee, careful to make sure it wasn't in any of the cows' runoff. "Do you know how they got sick?"

Jacques nodded but said nothing.

David smiled. "Can you tell me how they got sick?"

Jacques again nodded, and again said nothing.

David glanced up at Marcus. None of them had

experience with children, and they were all learning the hard way how to be caretakers to not only his niece and nephew, but the young Pierre. David continued to press. "*Will* you tell me how they got sick?"

Another nod but still silence.

"*When* will you tell me?"

"When you say please. Lady Joanne says we must always be polite and say please and thank you."

Marcus and the others chuckled, and David forced a smile. "Will you *please* tell me how the cows got sick?"

"Yes. They ate the shitting flowers."

"Huh?"

"The shitting flowers. That's what Father used to call them." He pointed in the direction of the pasture behind the barn, near the rear of the property. "They grow back there."

David cursed. "It's my fault. I moved them there yesterday to graze when I was cleaning the barn. It never occurred to me they might get sick."

Marcus dismissed his squire's concerns with a wave of his hand. "None of us could know." He pointed at the disaster that was the barn. "Do as the boy says. Use the hay to clean it up, then when you're done, go see Mr. Leblanc and ask him if he could come by when he has time from tending his own farm to point out what our cows should not be eating. I'd hate to see you have to do this again."

"So, you're not going to help us?"

Marcus grinned. "You know I would happily do so, but I'm going to Paris to meet with Sir Matthew."

A broad smile spread on Simon's face. "And of course, I must escort you."

Marcus shook his head. "Oh, I don't think that's necessary."

Simon's eyes shot wide. "I think it's absolutely necessary."

"No, I think I can take care of myself."

"You *think* you can take care of yourself, but you and I both know that you need me. The roads between here and Paris can be dangerous."

"I survived in the Holy Lands for over two decades with Saracens behind every rock wanting to slit my throat. I think I can make it a half-day's ride to Paris."

"I think you're getting foolish in your old age. You know you need me."

"I really don't think I do."

Jacques tugged on Simon's sleeve. "Say please."

Simon regarded him for a moment then stared at Marcus. "Please, let me escort you to Paris."

Marcus tossed his head back and roared with laughter, slapping Simon on the shoulder then tousling Jacques' hair. "Fine, you can accompany me." Marcus grabbed a nearby pitchfork and tossed it to Simon, then picked up one for himself. "But just because we're heading for Paris doesn't mean we get out of shit-shoveling duty."

Simon groaned as David and Jeremy grinned with delight, wisely saying nothing.

"Oh, my good Lord! What the devil happened here?"

Everyone turned to see Lady Joanne, ten paces away, a hand held up to her nose with Beatrice doing the same behind her.

"There's been an incident with the cows," explained

Marcus.

"Well, that much is obvious." She pointed at the pitchfork held in his hand. "Please tell me you weren't going to be foolish and help clean it up?"

Marcus spun the pitchfork. "Of course. We're farmers now. We don't get to pick and choose the jobs we do."

"On any other given day, that might be true, but we have to make you presentable for your meeting with Sir Matthew tomorrow, and we can't have you going in smelling like an outhouse, now can we?" She jerked a thumb over her shoulder toward the farmhouse. "We've made a hot bath for you and your sergeant. I want you in it now before the water cools."

Simon stared at her. "Together?"

"What are you, a heathen? The master goes first when the water is clean, then you go." She jabbed a finger toward the squires. "And when you're done in there, I expect you two to get washed up as well. It's one thing to suffer from the odors of a hardworking man, it's an entirely different thing to suffer from that godawful stench coming from that barn."

Simon turned toward the squires, smiling slightly at them. "I guess I won't be helping you after all."

Marcus slapped him on the back. "Nonsense. You can help them until I'm done with my bath."

Simon muttered a string of curses that would make a sailor blush as Marcus headed toward his bath.

"Don't worry, Sergeant. I promise not to take too long. No more than an hour or two."

More curses and beseechments to the good Lord to strike him down now, had Marcus laughing yet again. The children giggled as he headed to the farmhouse and the steaming bath that awaited him. He spotted Isabelle walking up the lane. She was a breathtakingly beautiful young woman who had been infatuated with him since she was a child, having built up an imagined future for the two of them based merely upon the stories told by his late sister.

His younger sister had helped build quite the fantasy, and when he, a monk sworn to celibacy, had spurned Isabelle's advances, it had devastated her. Thankfully, once she had met Thomas and had someone her own age to socialize with, they had quickly fallen in love.

Much to his relief.

"Miss Isabelle, it's good to see you this fine day."

Isabelle smiled then froze, her nose scrunching up. "My Lord, what's that?"

"Sick cows."

"Oh, don't tell me they got into the shitting flowers."

Marcus rolled his eyes. "Does everybody know about these things?"

"Anybody who owns cows in these parts."

"And do they have a proper name?"

She shrugged. "I'm sure they do, but nothing more descriptive. It's all my father ever calls them. Whenever he sees any on our property, he won't rest until he's pulled them all."

"Then perhaps you can tell my squires what to look for, so when they are done cleaning the barn, they can prevent any future issues."

"I'd be happy to." She stared at her feet. "Is it true you're going to Paris?"

"It is. We leave in a few hours. Do you have a message for Thomas?"

"Actually, I was wondering if I could come with you." She looked up at him, her eyes wide. "Please."

Jacques tugged on his sleeve. "She said, 'please,' Uncle. You have to say yes."

Marcus frowned at him then regarded Joanne. "I think you have a lot to learn about manners, young man."

Joanne frowned at him. "We haven't covered all the lessons yet."

"Evidently not. May I suggest the next one be why just because you ask politely, doesn't mean you always get what you want?"

"I'll take it under advisement."

Marcus regarded Isabelle and found he couldn't say no to her. "Very well, but it will be a quick journey. We leave today, stay with Thomas tonight, conduct our business tomorrow, then return the following day."

"No problem." She bounced. "I'll go get ready." She skipped down the pathway to the road, and his eyes followed her the entire way.

Joanne stepped closer. "You know, if you want one of your own, there are plenty of women who'd be happy to have you."

He tore his eyes away from Isabelle and stared at Joanne. "Excuse me?"

Joanne gave him a wry smile. "You monks are all the same. Celibate when there are only men around, but enter a pretty girl, and you're just as much a man as any other." She pointed toward the farmhouse. "Now, get washed up. You stink. Nobleman or not."

Lord François de Montglat Country Estate
Outside St. Denis, Kingdom of France

"Have you seen Madeleine?"

Lord François shrugged into his coat then glanced at his wife. "I sent her along with Jaqueline and Charlotte to the house a few hours ago to get things ready for when we arrive."

"All of them? You should've asked me first. I need help with the little one."

"I'm sure you can manage for a few hours."

Denise sighed. "You men really have no experience with these things."

"Considering I've helped you raise five children, I think I have more experience than most."

She gave him a look. "You provided for five children, but you certainly didn't raise them."

"I most certainly contributed."

She eyed him, saying nothing.

He waved a hand and surrendered. "Fine, you're right. I did nothing."

She reached out and squeezed his arm. "I wouldn't say nothing. You're more of a father to our daughters than most men, I know. What I mean is the day-to-day, the feeding, the changing, the cleaning. It just never ends. And as we both know, I'm too old for this. This is a young woman's game."

He stepped closer and put an arm over her shoulders, pulling her in and giving her a peck on the top of her head. "You're no old woman."

She wrapped her arms around him and rested her head on his chest. "Old for having young children, perhaps, but I'm certain I have at least a few more good years in me."

He laughed as he let her go. "More than a few, I should hope."

She sighed. "I look forward to the day when your duties at the King's Court are behind you, and I can spend my days with you by my side in our rocking chairs as we both go wrinkled and gray."

His eyes glistened. "A wonderful dream."

She patted his chest. "And now, thanks to you, we can pass on to the next life in peace, knowing our daughters will be taken care of by our new son should their husbands be unable." Her voice cracked. "You saved us all." She slapped his cheek gently. "But next time, you ask before you send my staff away."

He smiled. "You have my word."

She returned to busying herself with the baby as he stepped out of the room, his chest tight, his stomach filled with regrets. He was certain he had done the right thing. It was his only choice. Yet was it? Madeleine had been with them for years, always at his wife's side. She was fiercely loyal. Would she have ever given up the secret? He couldn't imagine it. The others had been with them for some time as well, though he couldn't speak to their loyalty. But was there another option? Could he have found them alternative employment, then if they had ever said anything, he could deny their claims as the ravings of angry former employees?

He closed his burning eyes as his heart drummed with guilt. His shoulders slumped. Even if he wanted to stop it, it was too late. A messenger at full gallop would take at least an hour to catch up to them. They would be too late, if it weren't already, and if he did send the messenger, he risked revealing the murderous plot he was involved in. He could lose everything after having risked so much.

There was no choice. He couldn't risk his family's future, not when his own was in doubt. He sighed heavily, shaking his head.

"What is it, dear?"

His heart nearly stopped at his wife's voice behind him. "Nothing, I'm just tired. I'm looking forward to getting home." He turned to face her, forcing a smile at the sight of her holding the boy.

"You know, we haven't chosen a name yet."

"No, we haven't. At least now we have something to do on the carriage ride back to Paris."

She beamed and kissed the boy, the boy who was his family's savior. He hadn't seen her so happy in years. He just prayed that the guilt he now felt wouldn't consume him for his remaining days, and the blood that would soon be on his hands didn't stain any future relationship with his family. He would do anything for his wife and daughters, and he had. He had kidnapped, he had murdered. What more could a man do to prove his love?

Yet the price he had paid was heavy, for while he had purchased their future on this earth with his soul, the eternity they were to spend together in Heaven was no more. They had done nothing wrong and would be welcomed by St. Peter upon their deaths, but his eternity would be spent in the depths of Hell, tormented forever for the sins he had committed.

En Route to Paris, Kingdom of France

The worried debate had gone on for the better part of an hour, Madeleine was certain. They were all in a whispered frenzy, everyone now convinced something was amiss. Her companions remained doubtful Lord François could do something so horrible, yet there was no doubt the mystery child had been kidnapped. She was certain of it. She could come up with no other reasonable explanation that explained the child, and the secret that must now be kept for a lifetime.

And if the Lord were willing to tear a newborn baby away from his mother, then what was murder to someone like that, especially considering they were all servants, people of no importance with no rights, one small step above slaves?

"I simply can't see it," said Jaqueline. "There's no way the Lord would do such a thing."

Charlotte shook her head vehemently. "You know as well as I do that baby isn't theirs. We all saw it with our own eyes. It was a girl and she was stillborn. Madeleine, you buried her for God's sake." She stabbed a finger in the air. "And there was *no* twin. You all know that."

Jaqueline batted her hand. "Oh, I don't mean that. Of course it's not their child, but I can certainly see them acquiring a boy to save his wife and daughters' future. I'm not excusing it, of course, but it's one thing to kidnap a baby and give him a future he could never have imagined, it's an entirely different thing to murder anyone who knew of the lie."

Madeleine regarded her. "Is it? You know how these people are. We are nothing to them. If one of us gets ill or dies or they're not happy with us, we can be replaced on a moment's notice."

"That might be true for us," said Jaqueline. "But the Lady adores you."

Madeleine agreed. "While that may be true, it doesn't matter. I don't believe for a moment she knows what her husband has planned." She lowered her voice in case the coachman could hear. "We have to save ourselves."

"And just how would you propose we do that?" asked Charlotte.

"We have to get out of this carriage and disappear."

"Disappear where?"

"Somewhere he can't find us."

"But where is that?" Charlotte wrung her hands. "I suppose I could go to—"

Madeleine held up her hand. "No, I don't want to know. None of us can know where each other is going. That way, if one of us is caught, the other two are safe. After today, we'll never see each other again."

Jaqueline, the youngest, her eyes bulging, sobbed. "I have nowhere to go! I'm an orphan. I have no family."

Madeleine reached forward and took her hand. "Change your name and head for one of the other cities. Go to a nunnery. They'll help you. You might even find another position in one of the noble houses there. Just make sure you change your name and never mention who you used to work for. Nobody can know, otherwise a letter might be sent."

Jaqueline sat trembling, wringing her hands in her lap. "I don't know. If we run away with no word, won't it simply make him madder? Perhaps it's better to speak to him and assure him his secret is safe with us."

Charlotte agreed. "She's right. Running away will just make it worse."

Madeleine shook her head in frustration. "Don't you two fools get it? There's a reason the three of us are together on our own. We're never going to see him again. We're never going to reach Paris." She held up a hand before anyone could say anything. "I'm leaving now. You're never going to see me again. What you do is your own choice." She reached out and gave both of them a squeeze on the forearm. "I love you both, and I pray that though we may never see each other again, that your lives are full and happy."

She rose and opened the door to the carriage, then jumped out. She hit the road hard and tumbled in the mud as the carriage continued on. She scrambled into the bushes that lined the road, then peered over the hedgerow, and to her dismay, saw a hand reach out and pull the door closed, her friends deciding to remain behind. Tears welled and her heart ached at what she was certain was about to happen as the carriage rounded a bend and continued out of sight.

She rose then checked herself. She was filthy, which was perfect. No one would pay her any mind in this condition, and she would be free to make her way back to the only other home she had ever known.

The slums of Paris where she had grown up.

Horses galloping behind her had her dropping to the ground. It was probably innocent, nothing she should worry herself about, however, the last thing she needed was some kind soul offering to give her a ride to Paris. The poor didn't generally own horses, so if word were to get around among the gentry that a woman had been picked up on the side of the road to Paris, it might make it back to her lord.

Four men on horses raced by. She stayed low, and was thankful that she did when she caught a glimpse of them through the brush. These weren't noblemen, nor did they work for any. Judging by the way they were dressed, they were ruffians, and she was certain they were up to no good. A lone woman like her found on the side of the road by men like these could expect a horrific end.

Her hand darted to her chest. Could Lord François have sent these men? Were they the ones hired to commit the dastardly deed, the ones sent to keep his terrible secret? Shouts ahead had her heart leap into her throat. Jaqueline screamed and swords briefly clashed as the coachman must have valiantly, though futilely, struggled to protect his charges. She made the sign of the cross, begging the Lord's forgiveness for thinking the brave man had been complicit in the entire affair.

Charlotte screamed, then Jaqueline again, their pleas desperate. Madeleine's lip trembled as she imagined what was happening to them. She pressed her hands over her ears, squeezed her eyes shut, desperate to block out anything that might provide her brain with hints as to what was going on just out of sight.

A blood-curdling scream from Jaqueline was abruptly cut short, then Charlotte cried, "No, please, no!"

And she, too, fell silent.

It was thankfully over.

Horses whinnied and hooves clopped, getting louder even through her covered ears. Someone screamed in the back of her mind. "Get down, you fool!" She dropped, realizing it was her own voice in her head. She pressed against the ground as flat as she could, and the horses raced past then faded into the distance.

She pushed to her feet, careful to make certain she was alone, then stumbled down the road toward her friends. She shouldn't. It was foolish, but she had to know. She had to know for sure. She came around the bend and saw the carriage in the middle of the road, the horses snorting, uncertain of what to do. The coachman lay slumped in his seat, his arm dangling over the side, his sword still gripped in his hand.

She ran toward the carriage, its doors opened, and climbed up, finding it empty. From her elevated position, she turned and gasped as she spotted her two friends lying in the tall grass nearby. She jumped down and ran toward Jaqueline, finding her dress hiked, her undergarments removed, and her throat slit. Sobs racked her body as she crawled over to find Charlotte much the same. She collapsed, draping herself over her friend's body as her tears flowed.

"We told them nothing."

She pushed up, staring down at her friend. Charlotte peered up at her, the light fading from her eyes as the blood continued to pulse from her neck.

"I'm so sorry!" cried Madeleine. "I should have forced you to come with me!"

Charlotte reached up and touched Madeleine's cheek briefly before her hand collapsed. "Run. Just run." A last sigh was gasped, and the pulsing of the blood slowed, then stopped.

Madeleine suppressed the desire to wail in despair,

and instead rose. She made the sign of the cross and was about to turn when she stopped. She couldn't leave them like this. The indignity was simply too much. She dropped to her knees and replaced Charlotte's undergarments then pulled her dress down. She did the same with Jaqueline. Whoever discovered them shouldn't know the final humiliation they suffered. The punishment for this was in God's hands now. And when those who had done this, including Lord François, faced their day of judgment, they would pay for their crimes on this earth with eternal damnation.

She rose once again, said a silent prayer, then headed toward Paris, the only life she had known for over twenty years dead to her.

En Route to Paris, Kingdom of France

Lord François sat in the rear of the carriage with his wife and their new son, his eyes closed as he struggled to come to terms with the horrors that were his responsibility. He could forgive himself for arranging the acquisition of the child. Yes, a family had been torn apart, but the boy was only days old, and though it would hurt for some time, those parents could have another child and move on, the compensation paid to them easing their anguish. The boy would never know what had happened to him, and would enjoy a life far beyond anything his parents could have provided. He would make sure the boy had everything he could ever dream of, the best education, the best prospects, and a mother and father and five sisters that would love him as if he truly were their own.

And without knowing, he'd be saving all their lives.

What had been done served the greater good, and perhaps God would find forgiveness on his day of judgment for the deeds of several nights ago. But there was no forgiving what he had ordered yesterday and that was to be fulfilled today. Until today, there had been no blood on his hands, but now, though he hadn't drawn the blade himself, he had ordered it, and he was as guilty as the men committing the dastardly deed.

The coachman called out to the horses and they slowed, the carriage coming to a halt.

"What's going on?" asked Denise.

"I don't know. I'll check." François opened the door of the carriage and leaned out. "What's happening?"

"There's a crowd ahead, milord, and a carriage is off to the side. The crest looks like yours, milord."

His chest tightened with the foreknowledge of what he was about to see. "Pull us over." He stepped out as the carriage came to a halt, his wife reaching for him.

"You don't think something happened to Madeleine and the others?"

He squeezed her hand. "Let me check. We'll know soon enough." He closed the door then his eyes for a moment, inhaling deeply as he steeled for what he was about to see. He strode over to the throng, several carriages gathered along with people who had been walking the road.

"What's going on here?" he demanded, assuming the air of someone who had no idea a tragedy had occurred. A man in fine clothing turned, and he recognized Sir Charles de Armagnac from the Court, cursing that it was him of all people that should be here. The man was a gossip, and word of this tragedy would spread through the Court like wildfire before nightfall.

"Lord François, I had feared the worst! Are you and your family safe?"

The question was reasonable, and he had to act as such. After all, it was his carriage, his staff murdered, and it was logical to think members of the family had been inside the carriage as well that could have been kidnapped. He gestured at the second carriage he had arrived in. "My wife and newborn son are in the carriage, and my daughters are in the city." He regarded the carriage he had sent his staff in, playing ignorant. "What's happened here?"

Charles held out an arm toward the field to the side

of the road and the crowd parted. François gasped as he spotted Jaqueline's body lying in the tall grass, his reaction genuine despite knowing what he was about to see. He rushed forward and made the sign of the cross at her slit throat. Nearby was Charlotte, also brutally murdered. His eyes burned and his stomach churned with what he had done, with what he was responsible for, then his heart nearly stopped with a realization. He spun on his heel, searching the area. "Where is Madeleine?"

"Who?"

"The lady's maid. She was with them."

Charles shook his head. "I'm sorry. I had my people search the area, and these are the only two, besides your coachman, of course."

He asked the logical question he already had the answer to. "Who would do such a thing?"

"Someone reported seeing four men on horseback leaving the area. Robbers, I would assume." Charles pointed at two indentations on the ground in front of Jaqueline. "It would appear they were raped."

François paled as he stared at the ground. "What would make you say that?"

"If their legs were spread, that's where the man's knees would go," explained Charles, his voice barely a whisper. "What I don't understand is why they would have put their clothes back on when they were finished?"

François' pulse pounded in his ears at the horror of it all. They were to have been killed swiftly and painlessly. What had happened here wasn't the deal he had made. He would never have agreed to these poor women being defiled in their final moments. It disgusted him. It enraged him.

Yet it was his fault.

He closed his eyes and gripped his temples, massaging his forehead as he pieced together what had happened here. Madeleine was missing. Now, with the evidence that these rapes had occurred, it had him wondering if they had taken her with them. He dismissed the thought. If they had, then certainly the witnesses who had spotted the men on horseback would have noticed.

But there was another reason to believe she had survived unscathed. Someone had attempted to restore dignity to these poor women, and it had to be Madeleine. If she had somehow escaped, it was exactly like her to return to check on her friends.

"My love, what's going on?"

He held out a hand behind him without looking. "Stay in the carriage!" he ordered his wife.

Charles stepped closer, lowering his voice. "I've already had a man sent on horseback to the city to check on you and your family and report the crime. You should return home with your wife, especially if your daughters are there. They will think the worst. And this is no place for a newborn. I will have the bodies and your carriage brought to your estate."

François stood frozen as the reality of what he had done set in. These three people were dead because of a secret he needed kept, yet it was all for naught. Madeleine was alive out there somewhere. She was out there with his secret, and she was no fool. She would know he had ordered her death along with the others.

The question was, what would she do now? Would she go into hiding and preserve the secret out of fear, or would she tell the truth and seek revenge? All he was certain of now was that he had made the situation far worse than it had to be. But there was no going back. Blood was on his hands now, eternal damnation a certainty. One more death would make no difference to the weight of the chains he would carry for eternity. He had to find her, and he had to silence her.

Otherwise, all would be lost.

Durant Residence
Paris, Kingdom of France

"Can I ask you something, Enzo?"

Enzo glanced up from a massive drumstick, his fingers and face greasy. "Of course."

Thomas wiped his mouth with a cloth napkin, his parents having raised him to always behave in a civilized manner, no matter their station. "What was the job that Mrs. Thibault refused?"

"What job? You mean the one that Passe thanked her for?"

"Yes."

"Why would you want to know?"

Thomas shifted uncomfortably in his chair. "I've seen Mrs. Thibault do a lot of things. I'm just curious where she draws the line."

Enzo tore another chunk of meat off the bird and chewed. He jabbed the air between them with the bone. "I can assure you of this. The line is drawn far short of children becoming involved."

"Children?"

Enzo grunted as he picked off every morsel of meat he could find on the bone that his initial attacks had left behind. "You wouldn't want to know what happens in these parts. Most people go about their days simply trying to survive. The stories you hear told that sound fantastic, that you believe are certainly lies, quite often aren't. When you hear a woman claim her baby was snatched in the night, or her child never came home from playing, it's easy to assume that she's lying, that she threw the baby into the river after her neglect had caused its death, or her husband had beaten her because they couldn't afford another child. But too often, the stories are true because people like Passe were hired to acquire something very specific."

Thomas' stomach flipped. "You mean people actually kidnap children?"

"Yes."

"But why would they do such things?"

"That, I *am* certain you don't want to know."

Thomas shivered. If Enzo were hesitant to give a reason, then it must truly be horrible, for he had seen disturbing things in his short time working with the enormous man and Thibault. He stared at his food, his appetite gone. "Are the children…" He hesitated. "Are they killed?"

Enzo continued to gorge, nothing affecting the man's appetite. "I'm sure some get killed, though that's not the intent, as far as I'm aware. All I can say is that they're never seen again."

"Does this happen often?"

"Just once is too often, wouldn't you say?"

Thomas agreed wholeheartedly. "Why doesn't anyone do something about it?"

Enzo paused, regarding him. "And just who would you propose put an end to it?"

Thomas leaned back and folded his arms. "I don't know, but somebody has to. These are children. Families are being destroyed."

"Families are destroyed every day in these parts. This is just another way."

"But that's different and you know it."

Enzo sighed. "Of course I know it. Which is one of the reasons I respect Mrs. Thibault so much, for she refuses to take part in it. She could be twice as wealthy as she is now if she didn't have her lines that could never be crossed. She really is a good woman."

Thomas suppressed his frown. While a part of him agreed with the sentiment, he hesitated to go so far as to describe her as a 'good' woman, though he wouldn't hesitate to say she wasn't entirely bad. She was complex. Very complex. The more he discovered about her, the more he was willing to admit Enzo was right. She had done many good things since he had been working for her, some even charitable, including funding the repairs on his family home after it had been set fire to. Yet not partaking, and putting a stop to something, were two entirely different things.

But Enzo was right. The criminals involved lived with no boundaries, and wouldn't hesitate to kill anyone who interfered with their business. And worse, those they were doing business with were nobility, untouchable by anyone except the King, and the King had proven time and again he couldn't care less about his subjects. For all he knew, the King could be behind the kidnapping, though he couldn't imagine for the life of him why.

But somebody had to do something.

A cheerful rap at the door had both of them flinching, visitors rare in these parts at this time of the day. Most people were in for the night, eating dinner, enjoying their time with family. Enzo held out a hand, indicating for Thomas to remain seated as he rose and lumbered toward the door. He opened it without fear, though his right hand was clenched, the resulting fist the size of a newborn's head.

"Enzo, good to see you're well."

Thomas broke out into a smile as he shoved to his feet, recognizing Sir Marcus' voice. Tanya burst into the house, tail wagging as she rushed to Thomas, leaping onto her hind legs and placing her paws on his shoulders, licking him with excitement. He closed his eyes and spun his head from side to side as he struggled to avoid the unwelcome affection, but found himself laughing nonetheless, for she was part of his new life, and the mere sight of her had him thinking of Isabelle.

"Leave the poor man alone," ordered Marcus, snapping his fingers. Tanya barked and headed for her customary perch in front of the hearth, curling up into a ball. Thomas picked up his napkin and wiped his face dry as Marcus and his trusted sergeant, Simon, stepped inside. Thomas leaned to his left then his right, hoping beyond hope that Isabelle was with them, knowing she wouldn't be. This was a business trip. Every month, Marcus was required to report to the headquarters, as he was still an official Templar Knight, though given special dispensation, along with his men, to be relieved of active duty so they could tend to Marcus' niece and nephew, and the growing number that now called the farm home.

Orphans and refugees of a failed system.

Isabelle wasn't behind the two large men, the confirmation leaving his heart a little broken. "Is Isabelle well?"

Marcus stepped aside. "Ask her yourself."

A sweet giggle that would melt any man's heart erupted from just outside the door, and his beautiful fiancée stepped into sight. "I am well, my love."

They rushed toward each other and he embraced her, hugging her hard, as she did him. He inhaled deeply, taking in her scent. He hated this time apart and couldn't wait to finally be married. Soon, they would be husband and wife, splitting their time between here and the farm.

He couldn't wait.

Activity below had him gulping and pushing her gently away. "It's so good to see you." He looked at Marcus and Simon. "All of you. Are David and Jeremy with you?"

Simon laughed. "No, they had a shit-shoveling problem to deal with."

Thomas groaned. "Ugh, the worst part of farming."

Simon slapped him on the back, nearly sending him to the floor. "You'll get used to it, my boy."

"I suppose."

"I see we've interrupted your dinner," said Marcus as Simon helped him out of his chain mail. It hit the floor with a thud and the two men reversed positions, Marcus returning the favor.

Enzo grabbed his jacket. "I'll go get us some food."

Isabelle gave Thomas a peck on the cheek. "I'll go with him, otherwise all we'll have is another bird, and Lady Joanne would chastise me if she heard I didn't make certain you had at least some vegetables."

Thomas smiled. "Hurry back."

"I will." She followed Enzo out the door and Simon closed it.

"That's a good woman you've got there."

Thomas had to agree. She was the best. She was

more than he deserved, and all he wanted to do was make her happy for the rest of her life, to start a family, raise children of their own, and someday, should God bless him with long life, meet his grandchildren. His face clouded over at the thought of his yet to be born child held in his arms.

"What's wrong?" asked Marcus, picking up on his change in mood. "Have we come at a bad time?"

Thomas shook his head. "No, no, forgive me, there's just something disturbing on my mind." He brightened at a thought. Somebody had to stop what was going on, and until this moment, he had no idea who that might be. But God had delivered once again, sending these two fearless warriors to his door.

Marcus finished stripping out of the last of his gear, then took a seat at the table as Simon did the same. "You look as if you have something you want to ask."

Thomas sighed then took his seat. "Something's happened, something's been happening, and I'm not sure what to do about it, or if anything even can be done about it."

Marcus folded his arms and leaned back. "Why don't you tell us, and perhaps together we can answer those questions."

Thomas relayed everything he knew from Thibault's encounter on the street the other day, to Enzo's statements, which were vague at best. Finally finished, he earnestly stared into both men's eyes, searching for any sign they believed him, that they were as concerned as he was.

And he found it.

In both.

For these were the best of men, who cared about all

God's children.

"Well, what do you think?"

Marcus frowned. "I think if this is true, and I have no doubt it is since Enzo says so, then it is disgusting. But before anything can be done, we need to know for certain that it *is* true."

Simon grunted. "From what I've seen of the nobility, I have no doubt it is. However, even if we were to prove it were so, what could we possibly do to bring an end to it?"

Marcus scratched his chin. "At a minimum, we could bring it to Sir Matthew's attention. As head of the Templar Order in France, he could relay the information officially to the Church and the King's Court. Certainly, those we know are involved here in the slums could be brought to justice, perhaps sending a message to any others who might think to fill the void. Without knowing more details, however, all of that is mere speculation."

Simon grunted. "And how would you propose we get more details? It's not like anyone's going to speak."

The sounds of Isabelle and Enzo returning had Marcus holding up a hand to the others. "Let's not speak of this in front of Isabelle. She'd be too terrified to ever allow your children to be here."

Thomas gulped and agreed. "But what are we going to do about it?"

"Tomorrow, we'll pay a visit to an old friend of ours and see what he has to say about the matter. If anyone would know, he would." He rose, as did the others. "But first, I must send a message."

En Route to Paris, Kingdom of France

Lady Denise rocked the baby, more for herself than him. He had cried from the disturbance after the discovery of the carriage and her dead staff, but had quickly fallen back to sleep, her soothing tones calming the poor boy. Though nothing could calm her. Two women she had known for years, two women, though servants, she considered friends were dead. Two women who under any other circumstance she would grieve as if a sister had died.

Yet this was different.

They had been murdered, and she had overheard the conversation. They had been raped as well. Her husband had said little in the carriage ride to Paris. Instead, she had sobbed alone, the baby comforting her as much as she did him. She stared at his rosy face, all scrunched up, as cute as any baby she had ever seen. She just wished he were her own flesh and blood. A bond was already forming, and she had no doubt in time she would love him just as she did her daughters.

But the lie would always be there, the secret would always be hanging over their heads.

He could never be told, he could never know, for if he confided in someone, it could be the end of everything for the entire family. No one could know their secret.

Her eyes shot wide and she stared at her husband sitting across from her. She bit her tongue, terrified of voicing the thought that had occurred to her. He was staring out the window, his hand gripping his prized dagger, his knuckles white. It was something he did when troubled, something he didn't even realize was a habit, a habit she had learned over all their years together. The question was what was troubling him. Was it the fact that three of their staff had been brutally murdered, and like any decent human being, he was disturbed by that? Or was it something more?

Only three people knew what happened that night, and two of them were dead. All three had been sent by her husband ahead to Paris, something that had never been done before, though when their daughters had been born, there had been no secret to keep. In the past, they had never left the city for their country estate after a birth, so there had never been occasion for the staff to be sent ahead to prepare the house for the arrival of a newborn.

She loved her husband and couldn't believe he'd be capable of something so heinous, yet she knew him. There was nothing he wouldn't do to protect his family, the proof in her arms right now. They had kidnapped a baby and she had agreed to it, not to save herself, but to save their daughters. Her brother-in-law was a horrible man, a hateful man, terribly jealous of his brother's position. They were twins, born only minutes apart, though her husband had been first, making him the eldest son. It was the law, and because of it, her husband had been groomed to lead the family, had the status, the title, the wealth, and his younger brother by three minutes had nothing but a promised inheritance from a man who would likely live as long as his sibling would, leaving him little, if any, time to enjoy whatever might be coming to him.

What her brother-in-law didn't know was that his

brother was sick. Her husband hadn't said anything to her, but over the past year, he had become frail, at least more than he should be at his age, and a cough had developed in the past few months. She had brought it up and he had denied everything. She had begged him to see one of the physicians available at the King's Court, and he had agreed. He had returned home that day subdued, though claiming he had been given a clean bill of health, but only days later, discussion began of what they should do if another daughter were born.

She had agreed to his plan to save their daughters from an uncertain future, for their fates would be in the hands of her brother-in-law should her husband's health fail before their offspring could be married. At first, when her husband had explained the plan, she had thought the very notion ridiculous, though apparently, it happened far more frequently than she would have imagined. Theirs wasn't the only family cursed with only daughters or no children at all. Some families lost their male heir through sickness or by accident, then mysteriously, within a year, the family would return from an extended stay in the countryside with a newborn child, always a male. She knew some of these families, and it shocked her when she pieced together the puzzle.

She agreed to the plan to save her daughters, her guilt partially assuaged by the fact they weren't the first nor would they be the last to do this. But secrets had to be kept, secrets that had to be kept for a lifetime, and she feared her husband had committed the ultimate sin to keep theirs.

He suddenly looked away from the window. "What was Madeleine's name?"

Her eyes narrowed. "Excuse me?"

"Her full name."

"Madeleine Rabot. Why?"

"And where was she from?"

"Paris."

"Where in Paris?"

"I don't know. The other side of the river, that much I know."

Her husband frowned and stared back outside.

Her mind raced, desperate for more information. "Why?"

He eyed her. "What?"

"Why do you want to know?" A wave of weakness swept over her, horrified she had asked the question, for she feared the answer would change their relationship forever.

He stared back out the window. "If she escaped, then she would most likely go back to her family. If we're going to find her, then we need a place to start."

Her eyes widened as bile filled her mouth. "Why do you need to find her?" Her voice was barely a whisper.

"To help her, of course. Whoever killed the others might still be after her. The safest place for her now is within our walls."

Her shoulders slumped in relief. It was a reasonable explanation and, despite having reservations on whether it was the real reason, it was something she could cling to for now, for though she loved her husband and always would, the thought she might be spending the rest of her life with a man who would have innocent women raped and murdered sickened her.

She closed her eyes and prayed, prayed for her

daughters, prayed for this little boy in her arms, prayed for the brutally murdered Jaqueline and Charlotte, prayed for her lady's maid of over twenty years, the best friend she had ever had.

And prayed for her husband's soul, something already lost to the Devil.

Something beyond saving.

Paris, Kingdom of France

Madeleine cried out with relief as she finally reached the outskirts of the city she had called home her entire life. The filth and misery housed within would hopefully allow her to lose herself among the suffering masses that made up the bulk of its population. She had left that life behind over twenty years ago, only visiting her family once or twice a year. Her parents were dead. All that remained now were some cousins, and a sister who resented her. If Lord François and his men were searching for her, the first place they might go would be her family, though she wasn't certain how they could possibly know where they were.

She could go to her sister's. It was the logical choice. Though the relationship wasn't good, they were family. Her sister had been jealous of the life she had made, living and working in a fine home, never wanting for food, drink, clothing, or shelter, always bringing them something whenever she visited, whether it was money or things no longer wanted from the estate. Though her sister was cold toward her, they had shared a tender moment last year when she sent word that their mother had passed. They had sobbed, hugged, apologized, and swore to be the best of sisters from that point onward.

Yet on the next visit, her sister was her cold self once again.

She had never told anyone at the estate where her sister lived, beyond that it was on the other side of the river. She should be safe there, at least for the night. She had to warm herself up, get some food into her, then make a plan after she got some sleep.

If her sister wouldn't welcome her, then so be it.

The sun was low and she kept to the shadows. It was some time into her journey to Paris before she noticed she was covered in blood, and she must make quite the sight. She had cleaned as much of it off as she could when she came across a creek, but the clothes were still stained. Her hands remained pink from the blood of her friends, clinging to her as if in a desperate attempt to stay connected to this world for as long as possible before the afterlife finally claimed them entirely.

As she pressed on, she received looks, for despite her state, her clothing was far finer than most she shared the streets with. Despite the fact that all she wore were the simple clothes of a lady's maid, they were in exceptional condition, with no holes or stitched together patches. It was clothing worthy of being seen in the home of a gentleman and by the guests that might visit him. She lowered her head and hurried along, avoiding eye contact, and as she thought about it, she realized it must be all in her head. A servant visiting family was not an unusual sight in these parts, and it was simply her paranoia that had her worried all eyes were on her specifically because they were all searching for her.

But that was foolish. Why would any of them be searching for her, especially so soon?

She turned a corner. Her sister's house was just ahead and she quickened her pace. She reached the door and knocked.

"Give us a moment!" called her sister from the other side of the thin walls. Footfalls echoed across the wooden floor. "Now, who would be calling at this time?" The door opened and her sister Grace gasped. "As I live and breathe!" Then her eyes shot wide as she stared at the bloodstained clothing. "What the devil happened to you? Are you all right?"

Madeleine burst into tears. "No, I'm not! May I come in?"

Grace reached forward and grabbed her by the arm, hauling her inside. She closed the door, but not before checking the street to see if anyone had spotted her. "What's happened?" she asked, her voice stern.

"You wouldn't believe me if I told you. And if I told you, it could put you in danger."

Grace's eyes flared briefly with fear and she glanced over her shoulder toward the back where her two children shared a bedroom. She gestured toward the bloodstains on her clothes. "Is that yours?"

Madeleine shook her head. "No, it's the blood of two of my best friends. They were murdered on the way here."

Grace's eyes shot wide and she paled slightly.

"They were going to kill me too, but I jumped out of the carriage just before it was attacked. If I hadn't, I'd be dead now too."

"But who would do such a thing?"

"My lord."

Grace gasped. "Lord François? But why?"

"I can't say. If I do, it will certainly put you in danger."

Her sister huffed. "I think I'm in danger enough as it is with you showing up here during the light of day. You should have waited until it was pitch dark."

Madeleine's shoulders slumped, her tears spewing forth again. "I know. You're right, of course. I'm a fool, but I was scared."

Grace's expression softened and she reached out, drawing her in and embracing her. It was a moment of comfort Madeleine desperately needed, and she clung to her, sobbing uncontrollably.

"Aunt Madeleine?" asked a young voice.

Madeleine sniffed heavily then wiped her eyes dry as she forced a smile on her face. "Yes, it's me."

Her niece and nephew sprang from the door and into her arms. She hugged them hard, thanking the good Lord that no one had ever taken them from their loving parents merely to protect wealth and position.

"Why are you crying, Auntie?" asked the elder Louise.

Madeleine laughed weakly. "I'm just happy to be here, that's all."

Grace snapped her fingers. "Back to your room. Your aunt and I have something to discuss."

"Yes, Mother," they both echoed as they gave their aunt a final squeeze before disappearing again.

"And don't be listening at the door!"

"Aww, Mother!" Footfalls had them heading back to the rear of the house.

Grace directed Madeleine to a chair and they both sat facing each other. "Now, you're going to tell me everything, right from the beginning, then we'll discuss it with Alain when he gets home. Together, we'll figure out what to do."

Madeleine nodded, then began the story of what had happened over the past few days, and with each word, her sister's jaw dropped further, fear filling her eyes as she finally understood the danger they were all now in.

Passe Residence
Paris, Kingdom of France

Passe glanced up from the coins he had been playing with. Nothing was more satisfying than gripping a stack and letting each coin fall, piling once again atop each other. The sound was intoxicating, something he would never tire of. He rearranged the coins neatly then leaned back as Lord François entered his office.

"I was wondering when I was going to see you."

François slammed the door shut, anger written on his face. "You failed."

Passe smiled slightly. "If anyone failed here, it was you."

This apparently caught François by surprise. "What the devil are you talking about?"

"You said all three of them would be in the carriage, but when my men arrived, there were only two."

"Nonsense. Your men are lying. I put all three in the back. I saw it with my own eyes."

"Well, there were only two when they arrived."

"Then she must have escaped somehow, and that's on your men."

"No, she wasn't in the carriage when they arrived. My men did their job. They eliminated the coachman and the women in the carriage, exactly as you hired us to do."

François glared at him. "You were hired to kill them swiftly and painlessly, not to rape them."

Passe shrugged. "Murder, rape and murder, what's

the difference? They used whatever technique they could think of to make the women tell them where your third servant was."

François' cheeks reddened. "And did they tell them anything?"

Passe frowned, flicking his wrist. "Nothing. The loyalty those women shared is remarkable. I didn't think women were capable of such things. So, now the question is, what do you want to do?"

"I want you to finish the job I hired you to do."

Passe regarded him. "We did. It's not our fault that one of your servants figured out what was going on and left before we arrived. Apparently, she wasn't as loyal to you as you thought." He leaned forward, his elbows on his desk. "As far as I'm concerned, the job you hired us to do is over. We eliminated the women that were in the carriage. Now, if you want to discuss the *new* job you have for us, finding and eliminating the one who wasn't in the carriage, I'm happy to do so."

François glared at him, then finally sat, the fight gone. Passe suppressed his smile as he leaned back, staring down at the man. He had him, and he could name his price, for this had gone too far. But what François didn't realize was this was only the beginning. He had his name, he knew where he lived, and he could blackmail him for years, though it wouldn't be for money.

Having a lord under one's control was worth far more than any gold. If he ever got in trouble with the authorities, if he ever needed a piece of information, he now had a source with a secret so great, any request couldn't be refused.

"Now, my men and I will be happy to try and track

down your missing servant and send her on to the next life so you may preserve your secret. However, that only works if she's in Paris."

"I'm quite certain she's in Paris, at least for now. She would have had to go on foot, and her family lives in this area. My guess would be that she'll seek help here, then either try to hide in the crowd, or gather provisions so she might escape to some other city to start a new life."

Passe's head bobbed. "Both perfectly reasonable assumptions. If she's wise, she'll leave the city as soon as possible. Remaining here would be foolish." He pulled out a piece of parchment and dipped his pen. "Now, what can you tell me about her?" He jotted down her physical description, a description so plain, it was unhelpful. "And her name?"

"Madeleine."

"Her family name?"

"Rabot."

Passe pursed his lips. "I've heard this name before. It's quite uncommon. That should help us. A name such as this will hopefully have us finding her family quickly." He put the pen back in its well. "Now, I have a question for you."

François frowned, folding his arms.

"What if we find her family and she's told them what she knows?"

François paled slightly. "I think you know what to do."

Passe smiled broadly. "Then it's settled. However, should we have to dispatch others, a premium will have to be paid."

"Of course." François sighed. "I just want this

matter over with."

"Good. Then, let's get this over with. I will, of course, require a deposit."

"Of course." A healthy purse was tossed onto the desktop, the rattle of the coins within sending goosebumps across Passe's body. He could tell by the size and sound approximately how much was in the pouch. "That's a good start."

François' eyebrows shot up. "Start?"

"Our job is much more difficult this time, and requires far more manpower. We have to find an unremarkable woman hidden within thousands upon thousands of other unremarkable women. Our previous job was three women and a coachman in a carriage that we knew the exact location of. The price will be triple."

The paleness of François' cheeks was overwhelmed with the red of anger as he sprang to his feet. "Outrageous!"

Passe shrugged. "You're welcome to take your business elsewhere. But I'll require that deposit in full before we begin."

"I don't have that with me, and we can't afford any delay."

Passe gestured toward a bejeweled dagger on the man's hip. "I think that should suffice."

François glanced at the dagger with an expression that suggested it was habitually there and he had forgotten all about it. His eyes flared. "That's a family heirloom. It's been handed down for generations from father to eldest son. It's priceless."

"And you'll get it back when you give me the rest of my money. And in exchange, we'll begin the search for your missing lady's maid at once."

François growled but unhooked the dagger and its scabbard, placing it on the desk. "If anything happens to that, I will send my entire guard here to slaughter every last one of you."

Passe chuckled. "I think you may find that more difficult than you imagine. However"—he reached out and picked up the dagger–"you have my word that as long as you don't betray me, you'll receive this back unharmed, so that you may hand it on to your eldest son that *I* provided you."

François stormed out of the office, once again slamming the door, his footfalls heavy on the steps. Passe carefully examined the dagger, the hilt gold with several strategically placed jewels, the scabbard gold as well with a fortune in diamonds, rubies, emeralds, and sapphires. He could retire off something like this, and he might yet choose to do so, but for now, he had a job to do, for he was a man of his word, and Miss Madeleine Rabot had to die.

Fortunately, unlike the old days when he was just getting started, he now had people to do the dirty work for him. His hands were never stained with blood, his knuckles were never bruised. He had always enjoyed beating a man to a pulp, though he entered every fight terrified. He was shorter than most. Not by much, but enough. His childhood had been made miserable, and men of greater physical stature had rarely treated him with respect. It wasn't until he had finally fought back one night at a tavern that he discovered his fists were like two blocks of iron. He had caught his opponent off-guard, knocking him to the floor, then wailed punch after punch upon the man until his face was bloodied and swollen.

And it had felt wonderful.

He had taken out years of frustration on the man, and from that day forward, everyone at that establishment treated him with respect, though it wasn't really respect. It was fear. What he hadn't realized at the time was the man had several girls working for him. Their protector had fled the neighborhood after the humiliation, and they approached him to take over his position. It was a dream come true. Money he didn't have to work for, and unlimited access to what the women had to offer. It had changed his life for the worse, some might say, though he would disagree. No one ever teased him, no one ever made any snide remarks. He had companionship and respect. What did it matter if the respect wasn't earned and it was merely from fear?

His first couple of years were spent beating customers who refused to obey the rules, refused to pay what was owed, and that was how he got into the lending game. After a good beating, many of his customers would beg for payment terms, and he would grant them at exorbitant interest, and soon the interest he was bringing in was rivaling what the women were, and a new business was born.

And his reputation and notoriety grew.

But once he could afford it, he brought in others to do the dirty work, for he was still a small man and always feared he would be bested by an opponent. His reputation could be destroyed or, worse, his life taken. Before it had all started, he couldn't care less if he died, for he had nothing to live for. But now he had the best life imaginable, and would do nothing to put that at risk.

He rose and hung the dagger on a hook on the wall behind his desk. It was worth a fortune, though no one would dare enter his office and take it. He headed downstairs into the large room where his men would congregate when they weren't out on business. It was time to find this Madeleine and finish the job he had been hired to do.

With her unusual surname, he had no doubt she'd be easy to find, and her time on this earth could be counted in hours, not days.

Trufe Residence
Paris, Kingdom of France

Madeleine sat at the table with her sister, Grace remaining in stunned silence, as she had since the story had been told. Fear was etched on her face, and it was understandable. Lord François had kidnapped a newborn baby, had a secret that had to be kept for a lifetime, and had ordered the rape and murder of the only people who knew. At this very moment, beyond the Lord and Lady, she was the only one who knew the truth, who knew the entire truth. She had to die to save the family. It was the only option he would be able to see, and she couldn't see him not searching for her until she was found and the danger to his family eliminated.

The front door opened and they both cried out. Grace flew into her husband's arms, sobbing. Alain laughed, giving her a hug. "Now, what's this?" He noticed Madeleine sitting at the table and frowned. "Please tell me you two haven't been going at it again."

Madeleine opened her mouth to defend herself when Grace pushed away, shaking her head. "No, it's nothing like that, my sister and I are fine, but something's happened and you're going to need to sit down and hear us out."

Alain's eyes narrowed but he removed his jacket and sat at the table. The two children rushed in to greet him then were sent away by Grace, disappointed that no dinner was forthcoming, the entire house filled with the enticing aromas of the stew cooking in a cauldron over the fire.

Alain regarded both the women. "What's so important that it has you leaving your husband and children starving?"

Grace reached out and gripped his wrist. "Once you hear what my sister has to say, you may find your appetite gone."

He frowned, then leaned back and folded his arms. "Then perhaps it's time you told me."

Madeleine began, with her sister filling in points she missed, and by the time they were done, Alain's eyes were wide, his mouth agape. He rose and headed for the door, opening it slightly then peering outside. He closed it.

"You can't stay here."

Her shoulders slumped, but her sister shot to her feet. "Of course she can!"

"No, she can't, for her safety and ours. If Lord François is searching for her, this will be the first place they'll come. We're her only family."

"But she hasn't told them where we live."

"Are you willing to risk that over the past twenty years, she hasn't forgotten that she mentioned it to someone? Or that no one saw her come in here on one of her visits? What she's telling us is that a member of the King's Court, a lord no less, has kidnapped a newborn boy to be the heir to his fortune, murdered three of his servants to keep the secret, and will just forget that she's out there? I guarantee you, Lord François already has people looking for her. They might not know exactly where this house is, but can she assure us that they don't know where we live?"

Madeleine stared at her hands, her voice subdued. "I never told anyone."

"Do they know you're from Paris?"

"Yes, of course."

"Then they know what side of the river you're from. They know you're from the slums, which is no doubt where the baby came from. If they acquired one so quickly, that means your lord has contacts in this part of the city, and they will no doubt be on the lookout for a new arrival who matches your description. Someone will no doubt remember your sister's maiden name, the connection will be made, and they will come here searching for you. And your lord will assume that you told us, and then we'll have to be killed as well." He pounded his fist on the table. "You can't stay here!"

Grace slowly dropped into her seat, pale. She stared at Madeleine, her mouth agape as if she wanted to say something, something too horrifying to speak. Madeleine reached out and took her hand.

"He's right, I can't stay here. I'll leave at once."

Tears filled Grace's eyes. "But where will you go? You'll die on these streets without any help."

Madeleine closed her eyes, feeling them burn. Her shoulders shook. "I don't know, but I can't stay here. We all must agree on that." She rose. "I'll leave through the back. If anyone comes here looking for me, you tell them I haven't been here, you haven't seen me since my last visit. Tell them you wouldn't expect to see me since we didn't depart on good terms. If they're well informed, they'll know that's true, as I've often spoken of our estrangement to the staff and to her ladyship, wishing things could be better between us."

Grace cried out and rushed into her arms, hugging her hard. "I'm so sorry we wasted so many years. It was all my fault."

Madeleine's tears flowed. "No, it was my fault. I'm the older sister. It was my responsibility to fix things between us."

Grace pushed away but didn't let go, staring her in the eyes. "Will I ever see you again?"

Madeleine shook her head. "No, it's too dangerous. I'm going to leave the city. I think that's the best option. I'll go somewhere where no one knows me."

"But what will you do? How will you survive?"

"Don't you worry about me. I'll make do." She broke the embrace. "I must leave now. I have no doubt his lordship already has people searching for me."

"Thomas Durant."

They both turned toward Alain.

"What did you say?" asked Grace.

Alain shook his head, breaking his distant stare. "Thomas Durant. I walked by his place on my way home. His friends are visiting."

Grace gasped. "You're not suggesting she go to him? You know who he works for! For all we know, she's the one behind all this."

Alain shook his head. "I'm not suggesting she goes to *him*. I'm suggesting she goes to *them*."

Madeleine's eyes narrowed. "Who are we talking about?"

"You remember Thomas Durant, don't you?"

"Of course I do. I used to watch him when he was a boy on occasion. I haven't thought of that family in some time. How are they?"

"The mother died years ago, as you know, and the father was murdered most gruesomely last year."

Madeleine gasped. "That's horrible!" She paused,

confused. "But how could young Thomas possibly help me?"

Alain shook his head. "He can't, but his friends perhaps can."

"And just who are these friends?"

"Templars with no fear of men like your lord."

Excitement gripped her. "Do you think they will help?"

Alain pursed his lips. "They might. I'll go ask them, but either way, you must make plans to leave immediately upon my return."

Madeleine rose and hugged him. "Oh, thank you so much! Both of you. I wasn't sure if coming here was wise, but you have both been so kind."

Alain gently pushed her away. "You're family, despite our differences over the years." He donned his coat and hat. "I'll be back as soon as I can."

Madeleine returned to her chair and sighed. "I never thought I'd see the day he'd help me in a situation like this."

Grace smiled. "I think his attitude toward you has always been a reflection of my own. With us now on good terms, then he feels the same way." She reached out and took Madeleine's hand. "I'm so happy we've fixed things between us. I only pray my husband can convince those Templars to help you."

Madeleine's shoulders slumped. "I, as well, otherwise I fear I'm not long for this earth."

THE LOST CHILDREN

En Route to Durant Residence
Paris, Kingdom of France

Alain Trufe stuffed his hands into his pockets. It was a chilly evening, the cold of winter still not out of his bones. Thomas' home wasn't far from here, and he set a brisk pace, wanting to limit the amount of time Madeleine was at the house. She should have never come. It was foolish and selfish of her to put his family at risk. A newborn baby had been kidnapped, three people were already murdered, and Lord François was clearly an evil man who would stop at nothing to conceal what he had done.

And now, he and his wife knew the secret. If anyone found out, they would be dead. He growled. He had never really liked Madeleine, though his attitude was tainted by the feud between the sisters that had been ongoing for as long as he had known them. At first, he had dismissed it as petty squabbling, though after more than a decade of hearing almost nothing but negative things, only ever hearing one side of the story, he had sided with his wife. Why Madeleine would come to a household where she wasn't welcome, where she wasn't liked, was beyond him. She should have never come, and he hoped that whatever came to pass, he would never see her again.

A man stepped out of the shadows, blocking his path. "Now, where are you off to in such a hurry?"

Alain's heart leaped into his throat and he stepped to the side, attempting to avoid the man. His accoster extended an arm, blocking Alain's path forward.

"Now, now, don't be rude. I have a question to ask. I'm not here to rob you."

Alain wasn't reassured, though decided antagonizing the man wouldn't be wise. He stopped, though didn't meet the man's eyes.

"Have you heard of a woman named Madeleine Rabot?"

Alain's eyes shot wide and his heart hammered.

"I see you know the name." There was excitement in his inquisitor's voice.

It was obvious this man was searching for his sister-in-law, and what he had feared would happen now was. His family was at risk. "No, I've never heard of her."

A knife glinted in front of him. "I don't like it when people lie to me."

Alain took a step back. The man reached out with his free hand and grabbed him by his jacket, hauling him closer. Alain cursed her for getting him mixed up in this. It was so selfish, so irresponsible. "I'm sorry, I didn't mean to lie," he mumbled. "I just know the name, that's all."

The man stared at him. "How do you know the name?"

"From the neighborhood. I've just heard it, that's all."

The man frowned, but let him go, the knife disappearing behind his back. "Well, if you or anyone else sees her, let them know that Mr. Passe is looking for her and there's a reward of one thousand deniers if you find her."

Alain's eyes widened and his jaw dropped. It was an unfathomable amount of money. He would have to work years to earn such a sum. The man shoved him out of the way and walked past. Alain stumbled toward Thomas' house as his mind raced. That amount of money would allow them to fix their leaking roof, to purchase cloth for new clothing, to dig a bigger root cellar. There were so many things they could do with that money, that it would improve the lives of his family dramatically, especially his children. He wouldn't waste it on indulgences like extra food—that would only help them in the short term. He would use every bit of it for things that would last years, such as the repairs to the house, better tools for his business.

He stopped. Thomas' house was just ahead. He glanced over his shoulder. The man who had accosted him was questioning someone else. It was only a matter of time before someone made the connection between Madeleine and her sister, then they would all be dead. He stared at Thomas' house and the fresh repairs recently made after the fire. He had helped in the rebuild, happy to do so, for he had known Thomas' parents, and his mother was a fine, decent woman who would be horrified if she knew Thomas were homeless.

What could these Templars possibly do to help? The more he thought about it, the more he realized all he was doing was passing his troubles on to someone else. And while the Templars might not fear Lord François or a man like Mr. Passe, what could they possibly do to protect Madeleine, and, more importantly, his family.

He closed his eyes.

Lord, please forgive me.

He spun on his heel and hailed the man who had questioned him.

Outside the Trufe Residence
Paris, Kingdom of France

Madeleine peered out from the back alley behind her sister's home. The sun had set now, and most decent folk were inside. Women of good character were only out after dark if it were absolutely necessary, for the streets were typically filled with men who had none. It was safer for all to be inside at these hours, behind barred doors, until the next morning when the light of day and the crowds that welcomed it provided the security in numbers from brazen attack. Unfortunately, it was those very crowds that could protect her that she must avoid—she couldn't risk being recognized, especially near her sister's home.

She darted across the street and back into the shadows. The Durant residence wasn't far from here, and though she hadn't been there in years, she could make her way with her eyes closed. She continued onward, ducking from building to building, her heart hammering with every sound, most of those still out hurrying home likely on edge as well. In another hour or so, it would be far less safe.

She wore clothing her sister had provided, her bloodstained maid's outfit feeding the fire. She prayed to God that no one came searching for her there, or if they did, that her family would be protected. Yet she had prayed a lot this day, and all had fallen on deaf ears.

She sighed. Perhaps they hadn't. She was alive, and she was supposed to be dead. Had God given her the courage to leap from the carriage when she had? She had always been taught that He had a plan. What was His plan for her that He had her surviving certain death? It couldn't be to simply live on. All she could think of was justice. God meant for justice to be delivered on this earth, and she was His instrument. If He did indeed have a plan for her, it was a remarkable one.

She had heard nothing but good things about young Thomas over the years, had even seen him on occasion when she visited. His mother was the best of women, and his father was a kind man with a sinful profession, a forger of remarkable talent. A criminal. How a family such as that could end up with Templars as friends, she had no idea. But for her to successfully deliver the justice she was certain God had saved her for, she would need help, help from someone whom the King and his court had no power over.

And in this city, that meant the Church and the Templars, and no one else.

The Church wasn't an option, since they had no means to effect any change should nobility be involved, but the Templars were warrior monks who served at the pleasure of the Pope, not any king. They were the only people she could think might help her.

The question was whether they would be able to. Her sister and brother-in-law had related stories about these Templars and how they were different than the others. They seemed too fantastic to be anything more than stories, yet stories like this often were based on kernels of truth. And something had to explain how Templars were such good friends with Thomas Durant, close enough to stay with him rather than at their mighty fortress when visiting the city.

That was perhaps the most remarkable thing she had been told. Never in her life had she heard of Templars in Paris sleeping at a private house. It simply made no sense.

Yet Alain had said they were willing to hear her out, to help if they could, and she had to have faith.

She reached the livery stable just down the street from the Durant residence and peered inside. There were several horses of questionable condition on one side, but on the other were three of the sturdiest steeds she had ever seen, and hanging nearby, fine saddles and equipment with Templar markings. Her heart raced and her eyes bulged as the stories her sister and brother-in-law had told gained credence. Templars must be staying nearby if their horses were stabled here.

A door opened and Madeleine ducked. The splash of a bucket of water being emptied had her hammering heart relaxing slightly. She continued forward, hugging the side of the buildings, inching toward the glow pulsing from Thomas' house. She stepped from the shadows to cross the street when a group of men rushed out from the other side, quickly surrounding her. A dagger glistened in the moonlight and she raised her hands, her entire body trembling with fear.

"Now, what's a woman like you doing out at an hour like this?"

She wasn't sure what to say. She obviously couldn't tell them the truth, and perhaps this had nothing to do with the events of earlier today, though being raped and murdered by these ruffians wasn't an acceptable alternative to mere certain death.

She made a decision and pointed at Thomas' house. "I'm going to my friend's house with some Templars.

They're expecting me."

The man with the knife smiled at her, revealing a mouthful of rotting teeth. "Is that what your brother-in-law told you?"

Madeleine recoiled in shock. "What?"

"I asked you a question, Madeleine Rabot. Is that what your brother-in-law told you, that the Templars were waiting for you?"

A wave of weakness swept over her, and she was about to faint before she remembered to draw a breath. A hand thrust out and grabbed her by the throat. Her mind began to shut down at the revelation. She had been betrayed by her own family. Her brother-in-law had returned from Thomas' only minutes ago, claiming the Templars were there and were prepared to help her. There had been jubilation between her and her sister, hugs and kisses exchanged, and goodbyes said.

Yet it had all been a lie.

He had betrayed her. But why? Why would he do such a thing?

"Say your name."

She stared at him, terrified, but said nothing.

"I won't ask you again." The grip tightened and she grabbed at his hand, clawing at it uselessly.

She said the only thing she could think of. "Charlotte."

The man lifted her from the ground. "I hate it when someone lies to me. So, here's what I'm going to do. You're going to tell me your real name, or I'm going to go and kill Madeleine Rabot's brother-in-law, sister, niece, and nephew, while you watch." He squeezed even tighter. "Now tell me, what's your name?"

Tears flowed as she pictured her sister and the children, all innocent in this. She closed her eyes, resigning herself to her fate. "Madeleine Rabot."

The grip loosened and she was returned to the ground, gasping for breath. "Very good." He grabbed her by the chin and directed her gaze toward him. "One last question. Your greedy brother-in-law claims he has no idea why you came to his house. Is that true?"

She hesitated, though only for a moment. While she would love to see her brother-in-law removed from this earth, his death was a package deal. She shook her head. "I told them nothing, I swear. You and I both know I'm already dead, and I love them too much to put them at risk."

He stared into her eyes. "If you love them so much, then why did you go there?"

Her shoulders slumped and her eyes closed, her jaw still gripped in his hand. He was right. She should have never gone. "Because I was a fool."

A horse approaching had one of the men hissing, "Someone's coming."

The man holding her headed into the shadows, dragging her along with him, a hand clasped over her mouth as the rider passed. Hot breath on her ear made her skin crawl. "It's too bad we can't take you," he whispered. "But when I slit your throat, know this. Your selfishness sealed the fate of the rest of your family. They won't see the morning sun."

A mix of rage and panic filled her. She opened her mouth, one of her captor's fingers slipping inside. She bit down hard, as hard as she could, and she tasted blood as he screamed. The horse whinnied and someone called out.

"Who goes there?"

The grip on her loosened and she ripped her mouth away, tearing the flesh from the man's finger. She kneed him in the groin and he doubled over, twisting away from her. She made it several steps before someone grabbed her arm. She struggled against the hold, the sleeve of her shirt tearing off.

She screamed. "Help! Somebody, please help!"

A knife shimmered in front of her as it swung, making contact with her cheek and slicing down the side of her face. The agony was unbelievable, and she prayed to God to end this one way or the other.

Lord François de Montglat Estate
Paris, Kingdom of France

Lady Denise handed the baby over to one of her servants, Blanche, who had been the lady's maid-in-training for several years now, the woman being groomed to replace Madeleine should anything happen to her. Upon their arrival, the household had been shared the truth, or at least the version of the truth her husband had concocted. Jaqueline, Charlotte, and the coachman had been murdered by ruffians on the way here, Madeleine had managed to escape and everything was being done to find her swiftly. If anyone knew where she might be or where she might go, they were to inform the estate's marshal.

And though Denise hadn't said anything to her husband, she was certain that if poor Madeleine were found by his people, she wouldn't live to see the light of day. He was responsible for this. There was no doubt in her mind now, but by agreeing to the deception, it meant she was as well. And eliminating any witnesses with knowledge of their secret was a logical extension of their treachery.

She was a murderer, a kidnapper, just like her husband. Though their hands hadn't torn the baby from his mother's arms, nor had they any blood on them, they were as guilty as those who had committed the actual deeds. They would both burn in Hell for eternity for what they had done. She squeezed her eyes shut as she sat on the edge of her bed, struggling to keep her tears at bay.

"Is something troubling you, milady?"

Denise shook her head. "Nothing that isn't troubling us all."

"Yes, I've heard of murder, of course, but never has anyone so close to me been a victim." Blanche finished changing the baby. "Would you like to hold him, milady?"

"Not right now. Make sure he's fed."

"The new wet nurse has just arrived. I'll make certain it's taken care of."

"Very well. Has my husband returned yet?"

"I'm not sure, ma'am, but I will check for you." The baby started to fuss.

"Get him fed. I'm not to be disturbed until the morning."

Blanche paused, confused. "And your husband?"

Denise thought for a moment. "Never mind about him. He'll see me when he's ready."

"Very well, ma'am. Goodnight." Blanche left the room with the baby, closing the door behind her. Denise lay down on her bed and curled into a ball, hugging her pillow as she gently sobbed. Why had they done this? Why had she agreed to it? The price was too high, yet until today, until the murders, she was convinced it wasn't. They had kidnapped a baby, yes, but it could be thought of as rescuing one from a life of misery and hardship. He would be loved and raised as a gentleman, a gentleman who would inherit her husband's title and fortune. He would want for nothing, and would have five wonderful sisters who would dote on him his entire life, and in exchange, he would make sure they were taken care of for the rest of theirs.

But murder was simply too much.

It was inexcusable.

She gripped the pillow tighter and sniffed hard. The deed was done—all but Madeleine. Her husband had left the moment they had returned, and she had little doubt it was to deal with the one loose end, the final thread of their secret that needed to be clipped short.

The one final murder.

She could demand her husband desist, but she feared it might create a rift between them, and if he were indeed unwell and his days were numbered, she didn't want to inflict any more suffering upon him. But poor Madeleine was her friend, the best friend she had ever had, despite the difference in their station. They shared each other's secrets, each other's troubles. They were as close as two women could ever be.

The friends she did have among the Court were fair-weather friends. All everyone cared about was their image. Nothing that troubled them was ever shared, no travails, not even illness. They and their husbands and their children could never be made to appear weak. Image was everything. They would have their tea, their cakes, gossip would be had about those who hadn't attended, the latest scandal of the Court would be chatted about, though only if it didn't affect any of the families of those gathered.

Their lives were façades put on for the benefit of others.

But Madeleine didn't care about anything like that. Her family was poor and would always be so. She didn't care about the comings and goings of the Court, the trysts, the scandals, the embarrassments. All she cared about was listening to the troubles of her lady and sharing her own.

She was a true friend.

Yet what kind of friend was she if she were willing to let Madeleine die to keep their terrible secret? She wiped her eyes dry and took a deep breath, holding it for a moment as she calmed her nerves. Madeleine could obviously never return to this household, not with what she knew, not with what had happened. They were beyond reconciliation. But Madeleine was nobody, and they were nobility. She could tell her story to as many as she wanted, and even if she were believed by the denizens that called the slums home, she could do them no harm. Even if word reached the Court, nothing would happen, for it would be her word, that of a servant girl, against nobility. And even if there were those in the court willing to believe her, nothing would be done, as too many had done the same over generations.

There was a knock at the door then it opened. She glanced over her shoulder to see her husband standing in the doorway. She rolled upright, sitting on the edge of the bed. "Where were you?" she asked.

"I had urgent business to take care of."

She didn't meet his eyes, instead staring directly ahead at the wall, fists clenched as they gripped the bedding. "Did it have to do with Madeleine?"

There was a pause before he answered. "It's nothing you should concern yourself with."

"I don't want her killed."

"What do you mean?"

"You know what I mean."

Her husband closed the door. "What is it you think you know?"

"You ordered them killed."

"I didn't."

"Don't deny it. You insult their memories by denying it."

He sighed heavily then sat beside her on the bed. "I had no choice," he said, defeated, his shoulders slumping. "The secret must be preserved."

Her heart ached with the confirmation of her greatest fears. There had never been any doubt, yet to hear it come from her husband's own lips was devastating. Her eyes burned and she turned to see his own tears streaking his face.

And she remembered why she loved him with all her heart. "This isn't us," she whispered. "This isn't you."

"I know." His voice cracked. "But it's too late now."

"We could give the child back."

He vehemently shook his head. "No, if we did that, then you and the children would be doomed." He sighed. "There's not enough time left."

She took his hand and held it to her chest. "Please tell me what's wrong. I know you're not well."

His eyes met hers, red, burning. "I don't want to burden you any more than you already are."

"I'm your wife. If you can't tell me what troubles you, then who can you tell?"

He smiled at her weakly. "I met with the physician at the King's Court, and he believes I have cancer, something very aggressive."

Her eyes closed and her head dropped, her forehead resting on his shoulder. She wasn't very familiar with what cancer was. All she knew was that whenever it was mentioned, it was also in the same breath as death. No one ever survived. "How long do you have?"

"He doesn't know, though not long. He suspects I'll be gone within a year at best, more likely months if not weeks."

She cried out in anguish, wrapping her arms around him, clinging to him. Yet it provided little comfort, his frame slight compared to the robust man she had married. He was a whisper of his former self, and now she understood his urgency. "What will we do?"

He patted her head, sighing heavily. "We'll do what we planned. All that I'm concerned with now is you and our daughters. That little boy ensures my legacy, ensures that this household inherits my title and lands, and protects you against the certain vengeance my brother would take upon my soul. I was the one who arranged for the child, it's my soul that will pay the debt that God will demand. He'll forgive you, for I would have ignored any of your protests, and you knew that, therefore had no choice but to go along with your husband's wishes. You knew nothing of the murders, therefore there is nothing that God will punish you for. Only I shall pay the price, but you and our precious daughters will survive and enjoy the long lives you were always meant to."

"And Madeleine?"

Another sigh. "She must die. I'm so sorry, but she's the only one left who knows the secret."

Her chest ached and a lump formed in her throat. He was right, yet he was also wrong, though for now, at this moment, all she cared about was the fact she might only have days or weeks left of life with her husband by her side. She collapsed once again into his arms. "I don't want to go on."

Trufe Residence
Paris, Kingdom of France

Grace sat upright in her bed, wide awake, tormented with worry over her sister. If something were to happen to her, she'd never forgive herself for having wasted so many years in a jealous rage. Her sister had never done anything wrong, and had made a good life for herself working for the rich, and she herself had a good life, though it was challenging at times. Her husband was a hard worker, and kept a roof over their heads, kept them fed, and had given her two beautiful, healthy children. Her life was as pleasant as anyone could expect in the slums, and she could have enjoyed it even more with her sister, if she hadn't wasted so much time with her petty jealousies.

And now she had lost her.

"What do we do if they come looking for her?"

Her husband groaned beside her. "They won't come. They have no idea who we are. Now go to sleep."

"How can you possibly sleep when men are after my sister?"

"Because there's nothing I can do about it, and there's nothing you can do about it. We've done all we can."

"But what do we do if they come for her?"

"How could they find us?"

"Well, certainly they know her name. If they ask enough people, they might remember what my maiden name is. That could lead them here."

Alain shifted in the bed, his attention finally caught. "You're right. Which is why you should have never let her inside."

"You would have me refuse my sister when she needed me most?"

He sighed heavily. "No, I suppose you're right."

She turned to face him in the dark. "We need a plan in case they come here asking questions."

"What did you have in mind?"

She chewed her cheek. "We could just say she never came here, that we haven't seen her."

"What if someone saw her. Then they'd know we're lying."

"You mean tell them the truth?"

"Tell them part of the truth."

She gulped as the situation became more real. "What partial truth would you tell them?"

"We tell them your sister came here, said she needed a change of clothes but refused to say why. You gave her the clothes, fed her. I came home, asked why she was here, she refused to say, then left. And if they ask where she went, we say she refused to tell us. She said it was for our own good."

Her eyes widened at the rapid, detailed reply. "You seem to have given this some thought."

He grunted. "Of course. It's my job to protect this family. So, are we agreed?"

She reviewed his story in her head then nodded. It was simple, it was believable, it didn't deny the fact they had contact with her sister, but it also showed they knew nothing of the secret. As long as they stuck to the tale, they would hopefully be all right. "I think it's a good story."

"Good. Then let us swear right here and right now, that no matter what happens, no matter what the threat, we don't deviate from it."

"What if they threaten the children?"

"It doesn't matter. The moment we admit to knowing what this is all about, they'll kill us all. As long as we give them no reason to believe we know why they're here, if we give them no reason to think we know anything, then they might just leave us alone."

Her eyes welled with tears. "Do you think they'll let us live?"

He embraced her and held her tight. "I'm sure they will."

"How can you be so certain?"

He squeezed her tighter, and his voice cracked. "Like I said, it's my job to protect this family."

She was about to ask him what he meant when he shushed her then lay back down. They held each other, and she slowly drifted off to sleep in his arms, nightmares tormenting her despite his warm comfort, when she was suddenly awoken by a crashing sound.

Alain was already out of the bed as footfalls pounded toward the room. Through the dim light, she could see him brace against the door, but he was knocked backward within moments as it flew open, several shadowy figures rushing inside.

And she screamed.

For God was not with them tonight.

De Rancourt Family Farm
Crécy-la-Chapelle, Kingdom of France

Every muscle in David's body ached. It had been a herculean effort, but the barn was clean once again, thanks in no small part to their neighbors. When he and the others had arrived last year, they had been greeted with open hostility. But once the misunderstanding had been cleared up, and through their deeds had proven themselves to be committed members of the community that could be trusted, the uneasiness shown toward them had turned into friendship.

One way Marcus had brought about this change of heart was to help the other farms when it was needed. Extra hands were always appreciated, and not a week went by where one of them or all of them weren't doing something at another farm. It made their own work that much more difficult, but yesterday it had paid off. Isabelle had told her father of their situation, and several hours later, half a dozen young men showed up for shit-shoveling duty. Everyone had toiled into the evening, getting everything cleaned up, and today's task, in addition to all their regular duties, was to rid the property of the shitting flower that had caused this mess in the first place.

A horse neighed outside their barracks and David exchanged curious looks with Jeremy.

"Did one of the horses get out?" asked Jeremy.

There was a rap on the door and David grabbed one of the swords leaning against the wall. "Not unless they've learned to knock." He readied himself. "Who goes there?"

"A messenger from the Templar Order."

David relaxed, returning the sword to the rack, though Jeremy stood by with his bow at the ready. "Enter."

The door opened and a Templar messenger in full regalia stepped inside. His nose scrunched up. "My Lord! When was the last time you two bathed?"

The string on Jeremy's bow tightened slightly. David decided a confrontational manner wasn't necessary, and instead chuckled. "You wouldn't believe the shitshow we had to deal with yesterday. Rest assured, we'll be bathing after today's chores are done."

The messenger laughed. "I have a feeling you might be needing that bath sooner than you think." He pulled a folded piece of paper with a Templar seal from his pouch slung over his shoulder. "Which one of you is the squire named David?"

David raised a hand. "I am."

The note was handed over and the messenger stood by, apparently instructed to await a response. His heart was pounding now, as squires never received messages. It had to be from Sir Marcus, which meant something had gone wrong. He cracked the seal and unfolded the paper, reading the message, thankful for Lady Joanne's lessons.

"What is it?" asked Jeremy, his bow and arrow now resting on his bed.

"Sir Marcus wants us to report to Thomas Durant's residence immediately. Apparently, there's a situation."

"I'll get the gear ready," said Jeremy, springing into action.

The messenger cleared his throat. "Your response,

Squire David."

"Tell Sir Marcus that we will be leaving immediately and should be in Paris by midday."

"Very well."

The messenger left, closing the door behind him, the sounds of him departing ignored as they set to work. Jeremy passed in front of him and David got a whiff of what the messenger must have experienced the moment he entered the quarters. He jerked back from the revolting odor.

"All right, we can't go anywhere before bathing."

Jeremy turned to him, tears in his eyes. "So, it's not just you?"

David laughed. "I think the two of us could take back Jerusalem by simply dropping into the middle of the city."

Jeremy roared with laughter.

David tilted his head toward the farmhouse that lay at the bottom of the hill. "You'd better request that Lady Joanne and Beatrice prepare us a bath. Also, let them know of the message."

"How long will we be gone?"

"It doesn't say, but tell them to expect us to return within three days, or a message will be sent informing them of our status."

Jeremy left and David continued to pack, his mind racing as to what could have happened in Paris that required their presence. It was obviously something dangerous, and something that didn't have to do with the Templar Order, for if Marcus required assistance, the Fortress was there with scores of men that would be available immediately. No, something had happened, something the Order couldn't be involved in, for the relationship between the Order and the King was tenuous at best.

Sir Matthew Norris, Commander of the Templar Order in the Kingdom of France, had explained that the Templars had lent a tremendous amount of money to King Philip to fund his military campaigns, and he was having difficulty paying it back. It was an embarrassment to the King, and a source of friction between him and the Order, as he had no power over them.

Since Marcus and the others had arrived from the Holy Land, too often they had become involved in the affairs of the King or his court, through no fault of their own. Marcus was a great man, a man who couldn't stand by while injustices were committed and the innocent suffered. David had no doubt that, once again, an injustice had been discovered and Marcus intended to deal with it. The danger didn't bother David. In fact, it excited him. The Holy Land had been a miserable existence, however they were always doing good, with potential battles around every corner, including ones of unimaginable scale.

Here, life on the farm was boring, repetitive, arduous, yet it served a purpose too. Three orphan children and two exiled women now relied upon them, and they were becoming a family, something he had never experienced before. If he were given the choice between staying here and heading back to the Holy Land, there was only one way he'd consider it, and that was if Marcus were going.

His loyalty was to him, not to the Order, though the two weren't in opposition to each other, for Marcus would never betray the Order. It was merely that the four of them had been through so much together, he couldn't imagine life without them remaining so. He could go today to the Templar Fortress and be reassigned to the Holy Land in a heartbeat, but he would never dream of doing so, not without Marcus.

The door opened and Jeremy returned. "They're working on it. Beatrice will let us know as soon as the bath is ready."

"Good. In the meantime, go tell Isabelle's father of the situation and see if he can arrange any help for the ladies to maintain the farm while we're away."

Jeremy disappeared again, and David resumed his preparations, heading to the stable to get the two horses ready, his mind once again racing, wondering what the next several days had in store.

Life might be boring on the farm, but the moment they stepped off, it never was.

Thibault Residence
Paris, Kingdom of France

Simone Thibault checked herself in the polished metal mirror, satisfied with the result. She should get herself a lady's maid. She could certainly afford it, but she wasn't nobility. Lady's maids were always from a different class. If they discovered intimate details of their mistress, high society would never find out, the secret effectively maintained from those it needed to be kept from, as there was no association. But here in the slums, any servant would be a neighbor who could then reveal to her friends and others the secrets and intimate details she'd been exposed to, and it would spread like wildfire through the community. Thibault would lose any respect and fear she had managed to attain. Chambermaids and cooks, those were fine, but the woman who dressed you in the morning, who helped bathe you? That was something entirely different.

Footsteps on the stairs had her inhaling contentedly. It would be Thomas and Enzo. A smile spread as the day was about to begin, and the only friends she had in the world were here to share it with her. Her little family was now complete.

She paused, her eyes narrowing. There were more footfalls than just two men. Her heart pounded a little faster at the thought it wasn't Enzo or Thomas at all. She stepped over to her dresser and pulled out a drawer, grabbing a dagger. She clasped the knife behind her back, holding it out of sight from anyone who might come through the door. If she were facing several men, her only hope was surprise. Whoever it was had to have slipped past the guards that watched the house at all times. Enzo was her enforcer, but even he needed sleep. There were always two men covering the rear and two covering the front, well paid for their efforts. If they had been eliminated, then this was a coordinated attack.

She eyed her door. The entire wall was reinforced, the door thick and heavy, with locks and a metal bar. It would take some effort to get through, and the moment they tried, she would be at the window, offering gold to whoever came to help her. She just wondered if anyone would take her up on her offer, or instead forego the reward to see her removed from this earth as the hateful person she would have them believe she was.

"Mrs. Thibault?"

Her shoulders slumped with relief and she giggled at the state she had managed to bring herself to. "I'll be there in a moment, Thomas!"

"We have guests, ma'am. Sir Marcus de Rancourt and Sergeant Simon Chastain."

Her mouth opened slightly at the answer to her panic, and she frowned slightly. She wasn't a fan of the Templars. Celibate monks only answerable to the Pope sounded like a bad idea to her, and their piousness was a constant reminder of her possible ultimate destination. But these two had helped her on occasion, and she them. What they had could never be considered friendship, though perhaps there was a mutual respect, but that respect certainly wouldn't merit a visit simply to say good day. Something had happened, and either they were here to inform her of what that something might be, or to solicit her help.

Either way, with the day mere minutes old, it had

already become interesting.

She checked herself once again, then returned the dagger to the drawer, shoving it closed. She unlocked the door and stepped out of her chambers, then headed down the stairs to her office. All four men stood outside it and bowed slightly. She suppressed a smile, for it always made her feel regal.

"Good morning, everyone," she said.

Her greeting was returned, and she regarded Marcus. "And why has the Templar Order paid me a visit today?"

Marcus bowed his head slightly. "Mrs. Thibault, the Sergeant and I are not here on official Templar business, though the matter is pressing. Enzo and Thomas thought you might be able to provide us with some information that might be helpful."

She eyed him, deciding to toy with him. "Information is rarely free."

He smiled slightly. "Unless given by a friend, to a friend."

She chuckled. "Are we friends, Templar, or are we rivals with a mutual interest?" She nodded toward Thomas.

Marcus shrugged. "The friend of my friend is my friend?"

She laughed. "I like the way you think. Are you sure you're a Templar?"

"As sure as anything."

She stepped into her office and sat behind her desk. Enzo took up his usual position in the corner, Thomas and Simon standing on either side of the door while Marcus took a seat in front of her desk. "Now, how can I help you?"

"I've come across some troubling information that involves children from these parts."

Her eyes darted toward Thomas then Enzo. Enzo nodded at her almost imperceptibly, confirming the topic concerned what she feared it might. She flicked a finger toward the door. "Enzo, stand watch. Make sure nobody comes up to disturb us. Thomas, close the door."

"Yes, ma'am," said Enzo as he stepped out of the room, Thomas closing the door before taking Enzo's customary position.

It was amusing how slight the boy was compared to her enforcer, so much more of the room visible behind him than when Enzo stood there. It was a position meant to intimidate those who sat in the chairs, the heavy breathing of the massive man a constant reminder that a good beating or worse stood only feet away.

But poor Thomas could intimidate no one.

"Please explain what you're talking about."

"Thomas mentioned his concerns last night that a baby might have been kidnapped in these parts, and Enzo indicated it was not an uncommon occurrence."

He paused and she suppressed a frown. There were lines in this business, some she was willing to cross, some she wasn't, and when it came to children, she never crossed that line. Unfortunately, there were those who would. She eyed the Templar, whom she knew to be pure of heart, and not one to stand by when the innocent were being victimized, though what he could do about this was unclear. "What do you ask of me, Templar?"

"I have a question for you." He leaned forward.

"And I must insist you tell me the truth."

She suppressed the urge to gulp, instead meeting his gaze. "I make no promises."

He peered at her intently, as if into her soul. "Are you involved in this type of business, dealing with the trade of children?"

Relief swept over her and she visibly relaxed, vehemently shaking her head. "I never have and I never will. The very idea is revolting."

He continued to stare at her before he gave a curt nod and leaned back. "I believe you."

"Didn't Enzo tell you as much?"

"He did, though I had to hear it from your lips myself. Are you aware of those who might?"

"Of course I am. I make it my business to know."

"Thomas thinks you might be aware of someone who recently committed one of these atrocities."

She glared at the boy. "What would make you think such a thing?"

Thomas paled in the corner, clearing his throat. "Our encounter with Mr. Passe the other day, when he thanked you for referring business to him."

Her eyes shot wide and her mouth opened slightly at the misinterpretation. "I'm horrified that you think I would be involved in such business!"

Thomas' jaw dropped. "I never—"

Marcus held up a finger, cutting him off. "Are you saying I've been misinformed, that this encounter never took place?"

She shook her head at him. "No, the encounter did take place. However, what was said between Mr. Passe and I has been misinterpreted. I was approached by a man a week or so ago, looking to acquire a baby, and I was immediately enraged and threw the man out of my office. In my anger, I might have mentioned Passe's name as the sort that would be involved in such things, and that I was nothing like him. It certainly was never meant to be a recommendation that should be followed." A pit formed in her stomach and she grabbed at it, suddenly feeling faint. "Oh Lord, a baby was kidnapped because of me!"

Thomas stepped forward. "No, ma'am, you mustn't think that."

Marcus raised a hand slightly. "I agree with Thomas. A person who is willing to kidnap a newborn wouldn't have stopped just because you said you wouldn't fulfill his request. This was happening no matter what you said, but now we have a lead on who may indeed be involved in this sordid business."

She processed his words. And the debate raging in her stomach settled, for he was right. A baby was getting kidnapped no matter what she had or hadn't said.

"So, you think it's possible that this Passe kidnapped a baby?"

She nodded emphatically. "Absolutely, it's possible."

"Are there any others who might do such a thing?"

Again, she nodded. "I can think of a couple, though I'm sure there's more throughout the city."

Simon cursed. "You mean you know at least three people who would do such a thing just in this area?"

"Within walking distance, I'm afraid."

Marcus exhaled heavily, shaking his head as Thomas slumped in the corner and cried, "We could be talking about dozens! Scores!"

Marcus was equally shocked. "Are so many children being taken?"

Thibault frowned. "One is too many, of course, but remember, these are people who are *willing* to do it. They're not likely doing it every night. I would guess we're talking perhaps a dozen people throughout the city who are heavily involved, and when someone wants something, they go directly to them. The rest are people who would do the job if they stumbled upon it."

Simon stepped forward. "That's a number we can deal with, but how do we find them?"

"How many of those you said you can think of would be among this dozen that we need to concern ourselves with?" asked Marcus.

"Passe and two others, and I can assure you they know who their competition is. Get one of them to talk, and you may get your names, or at least several of them, and then they may lead you to the others."

Marcus pinched his ear lobe, stroking it as she had no doubt he debated whether he should become more involved. It would be dangerous dealing with these people, for they all had men at their disposal, and no morals.

She leaned forward. "If you propose to do something about this problem and remove perhaps a dozen gangs from the slums, you aren't just dealing with the twelve men that are behind this, you're dealing with all their men as well. You could be facing hundreds."

Marcus' head slowly bobbed. "Yes, this is exactly what I'm thinking about, though it wouldn't be hundreds at once. We would deal with them one at a time."

She folded her arms and leaned back. "Would your Order help? You have hundreds of well-equipped, highly trained men sitting behind those fortress walls. Surely, with numbers like that, what you face would be an easy task to root out."

Marcus shook his head. "No, this isn't a Templar matter. They couldn't get involved in a thing such as this in the Kingdom of France. In the Holy Lands, absolutely, but not here, and certainly not with this particular king. I have no doubt he's looking for some reason to have us ejected from his lands, some reason the Pope couldn't possibly oppose. No, we will have to deal with this ourselves."

She eyed him for a moment. "You could always walk away."

Marcus' eyes widened slightly as he met her gaze. "Pardon me?"

"I said, you could always walk away. What concern is it of yours? These aren't your people, these aren't your children. You could walk away. Nobody would think any less of you."

Simon snorted like a beast behind Marcus, and Marcus raised a hand, cutting off any tirade about to emerge. "*I* would know, and God would know. As a knight, I'm sworn to protect the innocent and the defenseless. Who, pray tell, is more innocent or defenseless than children? They have none of the prejudices that plague men, none of the hatred. They're guilty of none of the sins that condemn our souls as adults. It is my sworn duty, not only as a knight, not only as a Templar, but as a Christian man, to take action. Knowing what I now know, I cannot possibly walk away. My soul would be tortured for the rest of my days on God's earth, then through eternity as I burned in Hell for the crime of just standing by and doing nothing when I had the ability to at least try."

Simon slapped his hand against his chest twice, rattling his armor, signaling his agreement with the words of his master.

She sighed. "Here lies Sir Marcus de Rancourt, who refused to just stand by." She regarded the man whom she respected more now than ever before. "I wonder how many tombstones have something similar carved on them."

Marcus rose. "Far too few, I fear."

She looked up at him. "What do you plan to do?"

"You're going to write down directions for where I can find Mr. Passe, then I'll pay him a visit later today. Give me the names and locations of the other two you referred to as well. But first, there's someone else I need to see, for his insight may be invaluable."

"Who?"

"Sir Denys de Montfort."

Her eyes widened slightly at the name. "Why would he prove valuable?"

"A man we assume is a member of nobility came to *you* seeking a newborn child. He didn't know you weren't in this business. That means he got your name from someone who also didn't know. That could be Sir Denys, who has a rather sordid reputation, and is aware peripherally of who you are. He is exactly the type that someone might approach for a name, and if it weren't him, he might know of others that might have provided it. Either way, at the moment, he's our best hope of finding out who came to see you, and who kidnapped a newborn child.”

Sir Denys de Montfort Estate
Paris, Kingdom of France

Sir Denys de Montfort sat in front of the fire, a blanket covering his legs and torso. He sipped a hot tisane, both hands gripping the cup, drawing every bit of warmth he could manage from it. His opium cravings had ceased, though his brief addiction had taken a toll on his body. He had lost his appetite for the better part of a month, and had taken to the drink to replace one vice with another before regaining control of himself.

He was eating again, and slowly coming to the realization that the life he had been leading, once enjoyable, had never been fulfilling, and certainly wasn't sustainable. He was now determined to regain his health, then begin a life that would have his parents proud. He wanted a wife, he wanted someone to share all that he had with, to fill his house with the laughter of children, to have what everyone else he considered men of character had.

Those without children, without wives, were the ones whispered about in Court, and that included him. One thing he had learned over the past year with his encounters with Sir Marcus and his band of Templar brothers, was that men of means and title had a duty, and that duty was to serve those not as fortunate as them, and to recognize the tremendous privilege under which they lived by the grace of being born to parents who had a title and wealth.

He lived a life far better than the vast majority of those who shared the bounty this kingdom had to offer, and if he continued in his self-indulgent ways, he would die alone with no heir to continue his family's legacy. All that he had would go to some distant cousin whom he barely knew. Perhaps that cousin would do something better with it than what he himself had done, but that wasn't the legacy he wanted to leave anymore.

Fighting side by side with Marcus, seeking justice for the defenseless and the weak, had changed him. Marcus was a far better man than he was, and had accomplished so much in his short time in these parts, merely by being honorable, merely by living his life by the code of a knight, and not forgetting the oath he had taken when given the title.

Denys had taken a similar oath when knighted, yet had done nothing but ignore it since the day he had discovered its trappings. There were plenty of women from noble families with little stature, desperate to land the heart and purse of a man like him. And then there were many women of ill repute, who couldn't be called ladies, that would fulfill any desire for a few coins. He had indulged in the pleasures of the flesh, of drink, and most recently, opium, shirking his responsibilities as he desperately sought something that would quench the thirst inside that craved contentment. He had always assumed sinful pleasures would be that source, would satisfy that craving, but it never had. Yet helping others had brought him a tremendous source of pleasure, of pride, of satisfaction in doing something good, and helping someone who wasn't able to help themselves.

And that was why he was determined to be healthy again, to be of sound mind, free of drink, to improve his reputation so he might attract a suitable wife and start the future he had only recently begun dreaming about.

There was a knock at the door and he frowned. He had given strict instruction to not be interrupted unless it was absolutely necessary. "Yes?"

The door opened and his chamberlain entered. "Forgive the disturbance, sir, however, you have guests."

"I told you I'm not receiving today."

"Yes, sir, however, I thought you might make an exception in this case."

Denys eyed his chamberlain, a man who had served him well for years. "And just who are these guests?"

"Sir Marcus de Rancourt and his sergeant."

A flood of warmth rushed through him at the mention of their names, a smile, rare these past months, spreading. "Show them to the drawing room. Get them whatever they need. I'll be down shortly."

"Yes, sir." His man backed out, closing the door behind him. Denys pushed to his feet, tossing the blanket on the chair, and set about making himself presentable. There was no hiding his gaunt appearance, his sallow skin, though he could at least make certain those things under his control were attended to properly. As he cleaned himself up, his mind raced as to why they were here. He liked these men, especially Marcus. It was refreshing to deal with people who had no agenda. While Marcus was nobility, he had no ambitions other than to serve his order. He wasn't one to play games, to scheme behind the backs of others. Denys never had to worry about whether Marcus was attempting to trick him or manipulate him, to use him to his advantage.

Marcus had helped him last year in the situation

involving Lady Joanne, and had saved him from certain execution. He was forever in the Templar's debt, and had helped him on several occasions, always to a satisfying conclusion, and it had him wondering what assistance Marcus sought this time. Whatever it was, he hoped it would be thrilling, for he hadn't felt so alive in weeks, if not longer. This was what he was missing in life, a purpose, and he prayed this good Templar was about to give him one.

He stepped out of his chambers then headed down the stairs and into the drawing room. He smiled broadly at the sight of Sir Marcus and his sergeant rising. Both bowed deeply. Denys returned the gesture, then waved his hand, dismissing the necessity of it. "We are all among friends here. There's no need for such formalities." He clasped Marcus' hand, shaking it vigorously. "It is so good to see you, my friend." He shook Simon's hand then indicated for them to sit. Again, they showed their deference to his position, waiting for him to sit first.

He leaned forward in his chair, his elbows resting on his knees. "To what do I owe this pleasure?"

Marcus regarded him, concern written on his face. "We've stumbled into a situation, and I'd hoped to seek your advice. However…" The Templar hesitated.

Denys leaned back. "However, you're concerned I am unwell."

Marcus nodded. "You appear to have deteriorated since we last saw each other."

Denys sighed. "I will admit, it has been rough, though my physician assures me I will make a full recovery." He waved a hand over his gaunt body. "What you see before you is merely the result of a lack of appetite, which I have recently regained, at least in part. Ridding my body of the horrible opium took some time, and unfortunately, I replaced one vice with another and took to the drink. I have since stopped that as well, and have begun to focus on myself and my well-being. If you had come here a week ago, I appeared far worse than this. Trust me when I say, I am on the mend, and in no time will appear my former self. I have learned my lesson, and the sinful pleasures I once participated in with such zealousness are behind me. In fact, I intend to seek a wife and begin a family."

Marcus smiled. "I am pleased to hear that, Sir Denys. I am certain you shall make a fine husband and father."

A warmth rushed through him at the words. "Thank you, Sir Marcus. From you, that is high praise." Denys turned to Simon, deciding to have a little fun. "And you, Sergeant. Do you think I'll make a fine husband and father?"

He noticed Marcus hide his smile with a turn of his head. Simon stared at the floor, then the wall, then the fire, shifting uncomfortably in his seat.

Denys leaned forward. "Well, come now, man, we're all friends here. You can speak honestly."

Simon cleared his throat and finally met his gaze. "I know nothing of such things, so my opinion is worthless, except to say, knowing what I now know, I would never want to risk bringing a child into this world."

Any joviality he had felt was washed away with the sincerity of the crusty sergeant's words. He turned to Marcus. "Of what does your sergeant speak?"

Marcus sighed. "He speaks of why we are here. We

have come across some information that is truly disturbing, and we were hoping you might be able to help us, for it is my fear you may have inadvertently become involved."

Denys' heart beat a little faster as he leaned back. "What are you accusing me of doing?"

Marcus waved his hand. "Please don't interpret my words as an accusation. As I said, I believe it to be inadvertent."

"Then perhaps you should give me some details that I can work with."

"Of course, sir. In the past while, have you had any opportunity to provide Mrs. Simone Thibault's name to anyone?"

A lump formed in his throat at the mention of the woman's name, and the blood drained from his cheeks. "Why?" he asked, his voice barely a murmur.

"A man, likely a nobleman, paid her a visit last week, seeking her services to commit a deed so foul, it's almost unimaginable."

Denys gripped the arms of his chair, steadying himself. "And what was this deed?"

"He wanted her to kidnap a newborn baby."

All strength fled him and he tipped over in his chair. Marcus lunged forward, his arm extended, and grabbed him by the shoulder, steadying him. "Take a breath, Sir Denys."

He obeyed, drawing several deep breaths, his strength returning. He heard the ring of the servants' bell as Simon beckoned help. The door opened and his chamberlain stepped inside.

"Bring some wine for your master."

Denys raised a finger. "A tisane."

Simon acquiesced. "Very well, a tisane."

"At once."

The door closed and Denys nodded at Marcus with a grateful smile. "I'm all right now. Please, sit."

Marcus returned to his chair and Denys gathered himself.

"I apologize for my display. I'm embarrassed you had to see that."

Marcus shook his head. "You have nothing to apologize for. We've all been overwhelmed at times. What is it about my words that troubled you so?"

Denys sighed. "I *have* given someone Mrs. Thibault's name within the past two weeks."

"May I know who this person was?"

He inhaled deeply, holding it for a moment. "I hesitate to say the man's name, for he is very powerful. I should have known why he wanted the name, but it hadn't occurred to me that he would do such a thing until you mentioned the kidnapping of a child, then it all made sense. If only I had known what he wanted the name for, I never would have given it to him." He shook his head. "I simply can't believe, though, that Mrs. Thibault would be capable of such a thing. I had assumed he was interested in drugs, or a mistress, or arranging for a theft. Never would I have assumed he wanted to kidnap a child."

"Yet you said it all made sense?"

Denys pursed his lips, his head slowly shaking. "The man is desperate. He has five daughters. His wife is pregnant with a sixth child, and the child is due about now. They must have had another daughter. If he did, he would be desperate to secure a male heir." He paused and stared at Marcus. "I suppose I still haven't said the name, have I?"

"No, you have not."

He sighed, closing his eyes. "Very well. Lord François de Montglat came to see me, and I gave him Mrs. Thibault's name, though not before I begged him to avoid anything like opium. It guts me to think I had any involvement in this."

"If he's that desperate, he would have obtained a name from someone else if you had not given Mrs. Thibault's. You are not to blame here. He is."

"And she."

Marcus shook his head. "No, she refused his request."

Denys' shoulders slumped. "Oh, thank God. I thought there was some glimmer of good in that woman's heart, and thankfully there might yet be. I fear for young Thomas' soul should there not be."

Marcus smiled slightly. "Mrs. Thibault is a complex woman with many layers, and in this case, she proved she has lines even she won't cross. Unfortunately, however, in her tirade directed at Lord François, she mentioned the name of someone who would be willing to cross the line, and it would appear that this man did."

"So, a baby was kidnapped?"

"It would appear so."

The door opened and the chamberlain brought the tisane Simon had ordered. "Sir, I hate to mention this, but Sir Charles de Armagnac is here. He appears quite excited by something, and insists on seeing you."

Denys frowned. "Do you have any idea what this 'something' is?"

"He mentioned it concerned Lord François de Montglat. Something of a most sensitive nature, apparently."

Denys exchanged a surprised look with Marcus, who subtly nodded. He had to take the meeting, he had to know what this was about, as it couldn't be a coincidence. He turned to his servant. "Tell him I will meet him in my office."

"At once, sir."

The chamberlain left, closing the door behind him. Denys rose, quickly followed by Marcus and Simon. "This can't be a coincidence. Something has happened."

Marcus scratched his chin. "Perhaps, though why would Sir Charles come here if something untoward has occurred?"

"He's one of the biggest gossips in the court, and unfortunately, I might be the biggest. If something has happened with Lord François, and Charles is aware of it, then he'll be desperate to share it with me. I'll see him, find out what he knows, then tell him I have other guests that can't be kept waiting."

Marcus bowed slightly. "Very well. But be careful you don't let on you know anything, especially about the possible kidnapping of a child. Depending on the type of man Lord François is, that knowledge could prove dangerous to you."

Durant Residence
Paris, Kingdom of France

Isabelle stepped inside her future home, directing Tanya to follow. "Let's go, girl. You've defiled the alleyway enough, I think."

Tanya gave one final sniff to a pile of garbage then jumped up the steps and into the house. Isabelle closed the door then walked through the hallway to the front, grabbing a broom. She was alone save the dog, and was on edge, though why, she wasn't sure. She had been alone here before, and with Tanya, she was protected. Perhaps it was the knowledge there were men on the other side of that door who would kidnap children that had her disturbed. Enzo had informed her what was happening on their way to get food last night, and though Thomas and the Templars had wanted to shield her, she had demanded to be included.

And now she was paying the price that knowledge sometimes brought.

With Thomas and Enzo at Mrs. Thibault's for the day, and Marcus and Simon off to see their friend who might provide clues as to who was behind the possible kidnapping of a newborn, she had to find a way to occupy her mind, and that was cleaning.

The place was a pigsty, at least compared to the home she intended to keep. It was bad enough when it was just Thomas, but since Enzo started staying here, it had become far worse. The man was a pig. Beatrice had said all men were pigs if left to their own devices. All one needed to do was look outside the walls of the homes that women cared for.

"The streets belong to the men, and they're filled with garbage, feces, and vermin," Beatrice had said one day. "I've heard tell that we once lived in caves, and I don't doubt that, though I believe it was us women that kicked our men out of them so often in order to clean, they built their own shelters outside out of necessity, not invention."

Isabelle giggled at what Lady Joanne had once said about the Templars. "It's not the smell of the men, but the beast upon them that troubles me."

There was a knock at the door and she froze, her heart leaping into her throat. Tanya was already on her feet, growling. Isabelle didn't admonish her, instead gripping her broom tightly as she tentatively approached the door. "Who is it?"

"Does Thomas Durant live here?" It was a child's voice, a young girl.

Tanya growled and Isabelle pointed at the ground, a child no threat. "You behave yourself." Tanya stared up at her. "Sit." She sat.

Isabelle opened the door slightly and found a boy and girl standing there, tears streaking their cheeks, terrified. She poked her head out and glanced up and down the street. Everyone was going about their business, paying them no mind. She opened the door a little bit more. "What are you doing here, children?"

"We're looking for our aunt, Madeleine."

"I'm afraid there's no one here by that name."

The two children exchanged glances, both sobbing anew. Isabelle opened the door all the way.

"You best come inside so we can sort this out."

They entered and she closed the door behind them.

Tanya gave them both a sniff then returned to her post in front of the fire. Isabelle sat them both down then took a seat across from them. "Now, why are you here? Where are your parents?"

"They're dead," cried the eldest, a girl.

Isabelle's hand darted to her chest. "My Lord! What happened?"

"Men came to the house last night. They were asking where Aunt Madeleine was and what they knew. There was lots of shouting then they killed Father and Mother!"

Isabelle's heart ached and her eyes burned. "How did you get away?"

"I took Monte out the back door and then we hid under the next house. The men searched for us but didn't find us, then they finally left."

"Why did you come here?"

"I listened to my parents and aunt talking last night. I know I shouldn't have, but I couldn't help it."

Isabelle reached out and patted the girl's hand. "I'm sure no one will be angry you did. Now, what did they say that made you come here seeking my fiancée?"

"My father said there were Templars at Thomas Durant's house who could help my aunt."

"Help her with what?"

The little girl shrugged. "I don't know. Something to do with someone named François."

Isabelle regarded her. "How did you find us?"

"Once the sun came up and people were on the streets, I just started asking people. I remembered Mr. Durant's name because I've heard the name before. I think my family and his were friends at one time. It didn't take long before somebody recognized his name and pointed us in the right direction. Eventually we found our way here."

Isabelle smiled. "So brave and so smart! I'm sure your mother and father would be proud."

Their faces clouded over with the mention of their dead parents. Isabelle wasn't certain what she should do, though she did know what always distracted children when they were upset. "Would you like something to eat?"

Another knock at the door had the children crying out in terror, her own heart threatening to pound out of her chest. She rose, her mind racing as she debated what to do. If men had killed the parents of these children, and they had asked perhaps scores of people where this house was, the murderers could have tracked them here.

She held a finger to her lips and motioned for the whimpering children to come with her as she headed for the rear exit. She eyed Tanya, still curled up in front of the fire. "Why aren't you protecting us, you mangy beast?" she hissed.

There was another knock.

"Mr. Durant, it's David and Jeremy. Are you there?"

She cried in relief as the mastiff's lack of concern was explained. She rushed to the door and opened it, throwing herself in David's arms, sobbing uncontrollably as her prayers for help were answered.

Sir Denys de Montfort Estate
Paris, Kingdom of France

Marcus and Simon both rose and a troubled Sir Denys rejoined them, closing the door behind him. He motioned for them to sit, then dropped into his own chair, shaking his head. "This is far worse than we thought."

Marcus leaned forward. "What have you found out?"

Denys sighed. "Sir Charles knows nothing of the baby's origins, but a healthy boy was born to Lord François in the past several days."

"You didn't mention our suspicions?"

Denys shook his head. "No, and I suppose it would be Lord François' word against ours if I did."

"Something vexes you. What else did you learn?"

"It is most disturbing. It would appear that the midwife and chambermaid, along with the coachman, were murdered on their way back to Paris yesterday."

Simon cursed. "If that doesn't confirm things, I don't know what does!"

Marcus held out a hand, calming his sergeant. "What else did he say?"

"He said he came upon a carriage belonging to Lord François outside of Paris. He found the coachman dead where he sat, and the two women raped with their throats slit lying in a nearby field. Shortly after, Lord François arrived in another carriage with his wife and newborn. They were apparently returning from their country estate. He was informed of what happened, and indicated that there was a third woman with them, the lady's maid."

"And they didn't find her?"

"No. Evidently she escaped."

Marcus frowned, leaning back. "Was there any indication as to who committed this atrocity?"

"Ruffians, it would appear."

Marcus grunted. "I suspect something more nefarious. If we assume that Lord François did indeed have a newborn kidnapped in order to have a male heir, he would need to keep this a secret, otherwise everything could be lost. The three women in that carriage were probably the only witnesses to what had happened."

"But what *did* happen?" asked Simon. "Can we be sure?"

"How many newborns were there?" asked Marcus.

Denys eyed him. "Just the one, I believe."

"Then that confirms it."

Denys' mouth opened in understanding as his head slowly bobbed. "You mean if that boy were indeed kidnapped, then the child that Lady Denise was carrying must have died at birth, otherwise there would be two newborns in the carriage, a boy and a girl."

"Precisely. And if their real child died at birth, the midwife would naturally be aware, and I'm assuming the lady's maid and chambermaid would be in the room at the time as well." Marcus shrugged. "I'm not really familiar with such things."

Denys waved a hand. "Nor am I, though I believe you to be correct. Then there's the fact that they went to their country estate so close to when the baby was due."

"Yes, that's curious, and I believe makes no sense unless we assume Lady Denise gave birth here, the baby died, then they headed for the estate where their kidnapped baby was delivered where there would be less risk of witnesses than at a large estate like here in the city."

Denys shook his head in shock. "They had it all planned out, right from the beginning!"

"You did say he came to see you a couple of weeks ago. I suspect he feared this would happen, so he arranged for a kidnapping, and when the baby died, sent word to have the plan executed."

"Disgusting!" roared Simon, leaping to his feet and pacing in front of the fire. "He must be brought to justice. Kidnapping a newborn, arranging for the murder and rape of two innocent women! He must be brought to justice!"

"Agreed," said Marcus. "Though I'm at a loss at the moment how we can accomplish that. We would need proof."

"Irrefutable proof," said Denys. "This is a lord of the King's Court. You can't accuse a man of his station of such things." He sighed. "But there is something else you must know, something that I fear precipitated this entire affair."

An eyebrow climbed Marcus' forehead. "Oh?"

Denys checked the room as if to make sure they were alone, yet still leaned forward and lowered his voice. "Serving justice only works if Lord François has a long life ahead of him that he wishes to enjoy."

Marcus' eyes narrowed. "What do you mean?"

"I mean, I have it on good authority that Lord François isn't long for this earth."

Marcus slumped back in his chair. "How certain are you of this?"

"Just seeing him would let you know something's wrong. He's deteriorated dramatically in the past several months."

Marcus waved a hand at him. "I could say the same of yourself."

Denys grunted. "True. However, when I was seeing the physician at the court to treat my own ailments, Lord François was there, leaving just after I arrived. He appeared quite troubled and shocked to see me, and left without the usual exchange. I asked the physician what was troubling the man and he refused to say what the ailment was, however, he did warn me that if I had any business with Lord François, I should conclude it soon."

A frown creased Marcus' face. "Well, that changes things, now, doesn't it? We can hardly threaten a man with justice who could be dead in months. He's more likely to redouble his efforts to kill the survivor so his secret is safe after he dies. Anything that might come out after would be dismissed."

Denys agreed. "There is no way the Court will declare the heir as illegitimate after death. Too many could face the same declaration if things were properly investigated. This has happened before, and it will happen again, as long as women cannot inherit. It is the dirty little secret of the Court that no one speaks of. I'm afraid we have little chance of bringing any justice to bear should he die before we have proof."

Marcus glanced over at Simon. "We need to come

up with a plan."

Simon grunted. "I say we slit his throat and take the baby."

Marcus chuckled. "We can hardly do that." He rose and Denys did with him. "My squires are due to arrive shortly and I have other business to attend to." He bowed. "Thank you, Sir Denys, for your assistance. It has been invaluable."

Denys returned the bow, clasping the Templar's hand. "I am always here if you need me. Let's hope we can bring justice in some form to this horrible situation. Perhaps then, people will think twice of kidnapping and murder."

"Let's hope." Marcus leaned in. "One more thing. Make no mention we were here. The Templar Order cannot become involved in this matter now that we're certain it involves an important member of the King's Court."

"Of course, my friend, you have my word."

Passe Residence
Paris, Kingdom of France

Passe sat in his office, Bertaut bringing him up to date on the previous night's activities. Passe shook his head. "So, you literally had her in your hands, and she escaped?"

Bertaut stared at the dagger on the wall, rubbing his bandaged finger. "Yes, sir."

"Despite the fact her own brother-in-law practically handed her to you."

"Yes, sir, but I cut her bad, I know it. If she's not dead already, she will be soon."

"Did you go and ask him where else she might have gone?"

"Yes, sir. He said he didn't know. We even tried persuading him by taking advantage of his wife in front of him, but all she would do is scream at him to not say a word and that they were dead anyway."

Passe grunted. "Well, she was right about that. The fact she knew it suggests that our lord's secret had been shared."

"Yes, sir, it's definitely possible, though they admitted nothing. Either way, their tongues are silenced, and I doubt they had any time to tell anyone else."

"Yet Madeleine has escaped, and so have the children."

Bertaut stared at his feet. "Yes, sir." His eyes shot wide. "Could she have taken the children with her?"

Passe grunted. "If she did, then she's the worst aunt ever, since she somehow lost them between her sister's house and Durant's."

Bertaut chuckled.

"We're going to have to find those children."

Bertaut stared at him. "But how? They're two kids on the street mixed in with thousands of vermin."

"They're two kids with no experience on the street. Talk to that imp Gerart. Have him spread word to the other children to keep an eye out for two new arrivals in the area who look out of place."

"How would they look out of place?"

Passe regarded his man. "They'll probably be the only two children on their own with clean faces. If we act swiftly, we can find them. In a few days, they'll be as dirty as the rest of the scum."

Bertaut smiled slightly. "Never thought of that. I guess that's why you're the boss."

Passe raised his fists. "These are why I'm the boss."

Bertaut gulped, having seen him in action. "Of course, boss. The Iron Fists."

"Have everyone start searching. Same reward applies. One thousand deniers to the man who brings me the woman or the children, and one thousand to anyone in the community that helps. I want them found before the end of the day."

"If the brother-in-law turned her in for one thousand, I'm sure the neighbors will as well."

"That's what I'm hoping." Passe eyed him. "Speaking of, I assumed you retrieved the reward we paid him?"

Bertaut's eyes shot wide and he reached into a

pocket, removing a large purse and dropping it on the desk. "Sorry, boss, I forgot."

"I'm sure you did." Passe waved a hand toward the door. "Now, get out of here. You're not searching if you're talking."

"Yes, boss." Bertaut left, closing the door behind him. Passe turned in his chair, staring at the dagger still hanging on his wall. It was worth far more than what Lord François owed him. He could pull the gemstones, melt down the gold, and buy his own country estate, though that wasn't how things worked in France. He needed a noble name.

Keeping the dagger, however, posed risks. François was very powerful, very wealthy, and no doubt had a substantial personal guard. They could come here, supplemented with the guard from the King's Court, and burn his house to the ground. Yes, he could reveal the secret, but would anybody believe him? If the dagger were discovered in the rubble, François would merely claim it was all lies told by a known thief who had stolen his priceless family heirloom. No, a secret like that was meant to be held over a man's head when something was needed, when the man was at ease, not fired up over an injustice.

Besides, his life was good. Yes, perhaps if he were to somehow acquire forged patents of nobility, it would allow him to insert himself into upper society. He might enjoy perks not open to him at this time, however he would lose too much because he would have to keep a lower profile. He would lose the power he now enjoyed, the fear in men's eyes.

Then there was the fact he'd never fit in with these people. They were a different breed. One dinner party, and everyone would know he didn't belong, and he could lose everything. But remain where he was today, and he'd have everything he ever wanted—wine, women, wealth, and respect.

He rose and peered out the window, staring up at the sun, judging the time of day. Midday was almost upon them. François should be here in a few hours with the rest of the payment. He smiled slightly. The agreement was if more people needed to be taken care of, there'd be additional charges. It might allow him to hang on to the dagger a little longer. He glanced back, the sunlight glinting off the gems. It was beautiful, and it would be a shame to sell it off piecemeal. Having it another day or two was a temptation that might prove irresistible, though it might be the only way to ensure François paid whatever amounts were owed.

He sighed then frowned. He was bored. In his line of work, most of the action took place in the evening. At least the interesting stuff. He had men out collecting on debts, women out working, children pickpocketing. It was an operation that ran all day and all night, for sinners sinned at all hours. But he was successful enough to no longer get his hands dirty unless he wanted to. He headed for his bed chambers then rapped out a coded knock on the wall, and within moments he heard someone coming up the stairs as he stripped out of his clothes. There was no better way to pass the time than with the comfort of a woman.

Or two.

He rapped out the same coded knock once again, and smiled as another set of footfalls rushed up the stairs.

En Route to the Durant Residence
Paris, Kingdom of France

Marcus rode back toward Thomas' house with Simon at his side. "I fear this is too big for us to handle."

Simon grunted. "Since when has that ever stopped you?"

Marcus chuckled. "True. But in the past, we could always count on our brothers."

"And we can't count on them now?"

"This time, we're going up against senior members of the King's Court."

"We've done that before too."

"Yes, but they were always committing crimes that would bring embarrassment to the Court. Bringing them to justice and allowing the King to then act upon it, as if he had no foreknowledge, meant we'd bring little to no harm to the Order. But in this case, it isn't one individual. There could be any number of noble families who have committed these atrocities in the past. Bringing this to light, exposing this secret, would embarrass the entire Court, and could irreparably damage its relationship with the Order. And if the masses were to discover what was happening, that their own children were being taken by the nobility, it could destabilize the entire monarchy, and our Order could be blamed."

"Then what should we do?" asked Simon. "Pretend we know nothing and return to tilling the soil and shoveling the shit?"

Marcus sighed. It was clear to him what his sergeant wanted to do, and it was the exact same thing he wanted to do as well. He had sworn an oath to protect the innocent, to protect the defenseless. This involved children, this involved newborns. He couldn't just let that continue. Yet what could he do? It was his word against a senior member of the nobility, and in the Kingdom of France, a Templar's word carried little weight with King Philip.

If François had indeed kidnapped a baby, there was little he could do beyond threatening the man to do the right thing, but with François nearing death, all leverage was gone. All he could hope to do would be to plead to the man's humanity. He might still attempt that, however, this was a man who might have ordered the murders of innocent women, and who had kidnapped an innocent newborn. He either never had any morals, or was so desperate, morality had left him.

"What's going on in that brain of yours?" asked Simon.

"Nothing much, I'm afraid. I fear Lord François may elude justice, as he is a desperate man with nothing to gain and everything to lose by continuing on his chosen path."

"Then we're giving up?"

"I didn't say that. We will meet with this Passe fellow, hopefully garner some information from him, and perhaps even persuade him to change his ways."

Simon grunted. "Wishful thinking, I fear."

"Agreed, though one can always hope. All I want to confirm is whether Lord François was indeed a client of his, and to know if he does this on a regular basis. If he makes a habit of kidnapping children, I'll gut him where he stands."

Simon smiled. "Now you're talking my language."

Sir Denys de Montfort Estate
Paris, Kingdom of France

Sir Denys sat by the fire, eating as hearty a meal as he had in weeks. He had been reinvigorated by the visit of his Templar friends, and his mind raced at the horrors that had taken place. Lord François was undoubtedly of a higher station, and a decade his senior, though the man had always treated him with respect, and had come to him in his time of need. It meant the man trusted him.

To a point.

His fear was where the killing would stop. At least three were dead already, and if the secret continued to spread, how many more would François murder in his desperate attempt to save his family?

He sighed. He couldn't just sit idly by when there might be something he could do to stop this. What that was, besides appealing to the man's better nature, he did not know. Not yet. But this was so unlike the François he knew. François was a good man, a just man, and he was certain this had everything to do with the death sentence handed to him by the physician.

François should have at least another good twenty years in him, by which time, with his family's good name, all of his daughters would have been married off, their futures secured by the noble families they had joined with, and by extension, Lady Denise as well. But if he only had weeks or months to live, only one of their daughters, Helene, was old enough to marry. She was a beautiful young woman, a woman he had met on several occasions as she had been shown off to the Court. He had delighted in speaking with her, and she had appeared quite smitten with him, though she was always off limits. He would never dare attempt to bed the daughter of a nobleman such as François, though as he had sworn earlier, those days were behind him.

A thought had him ringing the bell for his chamberlain, and soon he was on his horse with a small guard heading down the road to Lord François' estate. He was received in the drawing room after a short wait, and when François appeared, he was dressed for travel.

Denys bowed deeply. "I am sorry for dropping in unexpectedly."

François bowed slightly then dismissed the apology. "It's always a pleasure to see you, Sir Denys, though I'm afraid I don't have much time. I'm leaving shortly for an appointment that cannot be missed."

"Of course, of course."

François indicated for him to sit and he did, his host taking a seat opposite him. Denys regarded the man. He was a shadow of his former self, and the decline since he had seen him last was remarkable. This was a man who would appear as appropriately placed in a coffin as in a chair.

He was here to ask some difficult questions, and he decided there was no point in avoiding any difficult topics. "Milord, you appear unwell."

François regarded him, the bold question not something asked in polite company. It was evident that he wanted to say something, wanted to reveal his secret, so Denys took a chance. He leaned forward.

"François, I know."

François paled slightly. "What is it you think you

know?"

"I know that you're dying."

François appeared relieved at the explanation, and this revelation gutted Denys, for it could mean only one thing.

Everything else was true.

François had obviously feared he was aware of the kidnapping and murders.

"How? How do you know?" asked François.

"I don't want to say without getting anyone in trouble, but don't worry, your secret is safe, and I don't believe it has been shared with anyone else in the Court."

François sighed heavily, slumping in his chair. "It is true. I don't have much longer on this earth."

"There's nothing they can do?"

François shook his head. "No. The only question is, how much longer do I have? The only thing the physician could say with certainty was that it wasn't years. My time left is measured in months, perhaps even weeks or days."

Denys' chest ached at the revelation. "I'm so sorry to hear that, my friend. Is there anything I can do to help?"

François shook his head. "Beyond praying for my family, I'm afraid there's nothing that can be done."

Denys took a chance, perhaps a foolish one. "And your situation with regards to your heir, has it been resolved?"

François shifted in his chair, clearly uncomfortable. "My wife gave birth to a healthy son several days ago. Thankfully, the good Lord has taken care of that situation for me."

"Yes, the timing is most fortunate." He regarded the older man for a moment and François squirmed again. "What exactly was the purpose of your visit?"

"Sir Charles stopped by."

François groaned. "Then you know of our tragedy?"

"I do. You have my condolences on your loss."

"Thank you." François hesitated. "I hope I can rely upon your discretion."

"Of course you can." Denys lowered his voice. "I am concerned, however. With your staff murdered, do you think you are being targeted?"

François paled slightly. "What would make you think that?"

"It was a carriage with your crest. They would have no way of knowing it was staff inside and not you."

François pursed his lips, nodding slightly. "I suppose. I hadn't thought of that."

"And you approached me for a name of someone of, shall we say, questionable character. Could Mrs. Thibault be targeting you for some reason?"

François' sallow cheeks drained of any color they might have had. "No, not her. I mean, I spoke with her, yes, then changed my mind. I decided dealing with people like that wasn't worth it."

Denys smiled, despite the lie. "I'm happy to hear that. Sometimes no matter how far one has traveled down a path, it may seem as if you've gone too far to change course. However, that isn't always so." He leaned forward slightly and stared into the man's eyes. "You can always change your mind. You can always stop what has already been started." He paused. "You can always save your soul from eternal damnation."

François closed his eyes, his chin dropping to his chest. "I'm afraid it's too late for that."

A wave of weakness swept over Denys as the accusations were finally proven true. "What have you done?"

François drew a long breath then shook his head. "Nothing I can speak of." He rose and Denys followed. "Now, I have somewhere I need to be."

"Of course." Denys stepped closer. "You can always speak to me in confidence."

François regarded him. "I wish I could be sure of that."

He stepped closer still and clasped the man's hand. "I've known of your illness for months, and haven't told a soul. Should you wish to reverse the course that you have set upon, you can always come to me, and perhaps together we can find a solution to your problem." He paused. "And that of your family."

François opened his mouth to say something when he coughed, the single convulsion leading to a series of them. Denys helped him into his chair then rang for help. A servant appeared momentarily. "Bring your master something to drink."

"At once, sir." The servant disappeared and Denys returned his attention to François, whose mouth was now covered by a handkerchief. The servant entered a few moments later with a tray and several different choices. He placed the tray on the table and Denys grabbed a cup of wine and handed it to François. He took several sips between coughs, and his fit was soon over. He drew several shallow breaths, then a tentative deep one, and nodded.

"I'm fine. Thank you." He flicked his wrist and the servant retreated. He returned his handkerchief to his pocket, though not before Denys noticed it was spattered with blood. Denys stepped back as the opposite door burst open and the beautiful Helene rushed into the room.

He bowed to François' eldest daughter. "It is a pleasure to see you again, Miss."

She bounced on her toes. "I thought it was your men I saw out front! I would have never forgiven myself if I didn't take the opportunity to see you."

Denys placed a hand on his heart. "You flatter me, Miss, but it is I who would never forgive myself should I have not seen you this fine day."

She rushed forward and held out her hands. He gently took them and she curtsied. "I hope you're not just here to see Father."

"I was, though now that I hear you have a young brother, I believe it would be disrespectful not to pay my respects to the heir to the de Montglat legacy."

"Oh, you should see him. He's precious!" She turned to her father. "May I show him the baby?"

François snapped his fingers and his chamberlain appeared. "Get one of the maids to chaperone these two. Sir Denys wishes to pay his respects to my son."

"At once, milord."

"Wait until you see him. He's so adorable! He almost didn't make it, you know. I thought he had died at birth, but I was wrong. It was his twin sister. Everyone kept him a secret because they feared he wouldn't make it either, but within a couple of days, he was fine. Thank the good Lord, He's saved us all from my wretched uncle."

François cleared his throat. "You know better than to speak of family matters in front of others."

Her cheeks flushed. "Of course, Father. I apologize."

"We all have family we don't get along with," said Denys. "Most of my family rarely speaks to me anymore after the questionable choices I've made in my youth, but recent events have taught me a valuable lesson and I have sworn to change for the better."

She squeezed his hands tightly. "That is wonderful news! And does this new life have any specific plans?"

He smiled at her, losing himself in her eyes, almost forgetting that her father stood not three paces away. "I intend to find myself a good wife, start a family, and create a life for myself that I can be proud of."

Her cheeks flushed and she stared at her feet. "And have you chosen this wife?"

He tossed his head back and laughed. "No, I only made this decision this morning, but I can say that if she's half as lovely as you, then I would be a lucky man until the day I died."

The door opened and a maid entered, François grunting. "Just in time."

Denys let go of Helene's hands and turned to face François. He bowed and François returned the gesture, then leaned closer.

"I expect you to be an honorable man."

Denys nodded. "You have my word, Lord François, that I have nothing but the best of intentions toward your family, and will always be there to help them and yourself in your time of need." He stepped closer. "No matter what it is you may need help getting out of."

François regarded him, clearly troubled. He opened

his mouth to say something then stopped, glancing at his excited daughter. "I'm afraid I must take my leave." He spun on his heel and swiftly left the room.

Helene grabbed Denys' arm as the maid watched on with what appeared to be a permanent frown creasing her face. He didn't blame her. If she knew anything of his past, a past that had only ended this morning, her disapproval was warranted.

As Helene led him upstairs, she gushed about the newborn and the horrors of the night he had been born, unintentionally revealing little tidbits that, in the context he now knew was the truth, confirmed, in his mind, his worst fears. A baby had been stillborn that night, and no twin had been born. If a sickly baby had been, and it were a boy, the desperately needed male heir would be the most important birth in the Kingdom this year, and he would have been rushed to a physician to make certain he had every chance at survival, not taken to the countryside in an hours long carriage ride.

It was devastating to think of, and he wondered what he would do if he were in François' situation with a wife and five daughters, and the male heir to the family fortune so wickedly estranged.

He might do the same.

The wet nurse handed over the baby and Helene held him in her arms, beaming. It was clear to Denys that she had no idea that this wasn't her brother, that this baby represented her father selling his soul to save her and the rest of her family from an uncertain future. She stared up at him, her face so fresh, so full of life, so beautiful. It had him wondering what life would be like to have his own child, and the very notion filled him with joy.

"Do you want to hold him?"

His eyes shot wide and he shook his head. "I've never held a baby before, and I'm certainly not going to start with the heir to your family. I'm liable to drop him."

The wet nurse's eyes shot wide and she rushed forward. "Perhaps I should finish feeding him." The concern on her face was evident, this woman clearly aware of how important the child was to the family. They left the room, Helene once again clasping his arm, the maid trailing them down the hallway toward the front entrance.

"I would have you pay your respects to Mother, however, we've suffered a tragedy."

It was the first time her mood wasn't content. He was aware of the reason, however played ignorant. "Of what tragedy do you speak?"

"Yesterday, several of our staff were sent back from the country estate to ready things for my parents' return with the baby. The carriage was attacked."

He stopped and turned to face her, taking her hands in his. The maid cleared her throat and he gave her a sideways glance, the woman shrugging and tossing up her hands as if to ask what else did he expect—she was only following orders. He ignored her. "Was anyone hurt?"

Tears filled Helene's eyes. "The coachman, chambermaid, and midwife were killed, and the lady's maid who was with my mother for over twenty years is missing. My father has people out looking for her, but he's not optimistic. He said to prepare ourselves for more bad news." Tears rolled down her cheeks. "Who could do something so cruel?"

He desperately wanted to tell this poor innocent girl that it was her father who had done this, yet he couldn't devastate her. And while her father should burn in Hell for what he had done, the family didn't deserve to suffer. He suppressed a frown. So many innocent people were involved here, it was soul-crushing.

"I'm terribly sorry to hear that," he said, clasping her hands to his chest. "The world can be a cruel place."

The maid cleared her throat once again and Helene rolled her eyes at him. He winked at her, making certain to do so with the eye hidden from their chaperone. He lowered his voice as she wiped her cheeks dry. "Would you do me the honor of letting me call on you again?"

Her cheeks flushed and her eyes widened as any thought that had troubled her was forgotten. "I would be most agreeable to that!" She bounced several times on her toes. "I would have to, of course, get permission from Mother and Father, and if they agreed, then of course you would have to speak with my father."

He sighed, tilting his head slightly. "Well, then, we don't stand a chance, now, do we?"

Her eyes narrowed. "Why is that?"

He leaned forward and whispered in her ear. "Because I'm known as a bit of a scoundrel."

She giggled. "I'm sure you exaggerate."

He put a little distance between them, the maid glaring from the corner of his eye. "I don't, though I have vowed to change my ways."

She swung her heel, one toe on the ground as she stared at the hand he still clasped. "Perhaps I can help you restore your reputation."

He smiled and reached out, tilting up her chin so their eyes could meet. "If anyone can, it's you." They stared at each other for a moment, then hands clapped briskly three times.

"Enough of that! The gentleman has seen the baby. Should he want to spend more time with you, then it will only be with the permission of the Lord and Lady."

Denys turned toward her and bowed deeply. "You're a credit to the household, miss, protecting the virtue of this young woman." He turned to Helene and bowed, giving the top of her hand a gentle, lingering kiss. "I look forward until the next time we meet."

She flushed. "As do I."

He left the impressive estate, riding back toward his own, his heart as light as it had ever felt. He had been in love before, though it had been a lie, a lie that had devastated him so terribly, the wounds were still fresh. But now he felt a renewed sense of purpose. He had vowed just this day to turn his life around, and just those few moments with the lovely Helene had given him hope. While there was no way François would allow him to court the eldest daughter of the household, it was heartening to think that there were beautiful, young, intelligent women out there from good families who would consider him.

He sighed as they reached his estate. Though not as impressive as François', it was still notable nonetheless. He dismounted with renewed vigor and entered the house, calling for a meal to be prepared. If he were to restore his good name with the King's Court and the families of the daughters that might be seeking husbands of his stature, he would need his strength back, and he would certainly need to appear far healthier than he did now.

He smiled as he thought of Helene and the moment

they had shared, then tossed his head back and laughed heartily at what François' reaction would be should he request permission to court his daughter.

But he didn't have to imagine, for he was determined to ask him before it was too late.

En Route to Durant Residence
Paris, Kingdom of France

Marcus rounded the final bend, Thomas' house just ahead. He spotted two horses with Templar markings in front and he tensed. He had no doubt they belonged to his squires, David and Jeremy. The question was why they hadn't stabled the beasts upon arrival.

"Check the roof," said Simon.

Marcus directed his attention and urged his horse faster at the sight of David, bow and arrow in hand, on the rooftop. "Something's wrong."

David spotted them approaching and waved, then disappeared as they pulled up to the house and tied up their horses. He knocked on the front door and it immediately opened, Jeremy standing there.

"Sir Marcus, thank God you're here!"

Marcus and Simon entered and Jeremy poked his head outside before closing the door.

"What's happened here?" asked Marcus as he saw the room. Isabelle was sitting in a chair at the table, two young children he didn't recognize hugging her, all three of them with stained cheeks, though no longer crying. Their exhaustion suggested they had been sobbing for some time.

"There's been an incident," said David as he entered the room. "Perhaps Miss Isabelle should explain."

Isabelle appeared horrified at the idea, though eventually sighed. "After you left this morning, these two children knocked on the door."

Marcus didn't like where this was going, though he said nothing, allowing Isabelle to continue for as long as she could before the tears that threatened to erupt finally did so. "Apparently, men came into their house in the middle of the night." She lowered her voice. "And murdered their parents."

Marcus suppressed a curse. "Why did they come here?"

"They were looking for their aunt who they thought had come here last night."

"Oh?"

"Yes, apparently she was coming here to see you."

Marcus' eyebrows shot up. "Me?" He took a seat at the table, smiling at the children. "I'm Marcus. What are your names?"

"I'm Louise," said the girl. "This is my brother Monte."

"And the name of your aunt?"

"Aunt Madeleine."

"Do you know her last name?"

Louise shook her head.

"That's fine." Marcus leaned in closer. "Now, do you know why your aunt was coming to see me?"

"Something to do with a man named François. That's all I know."

Simon cursed in the corner and Marcus rose, suppressing the shock. He joined his sergeant and squires.

"There's no way that's a coincidence," said Simon.

Marcus agreed. He turned to Louise. "What sort of work does your aunt do?"

"She's a lady's maid," beamed Louise. "She's very

important."

"Thank you, dear." Marcus turned back to his men. "This Madeleine has to be the missing lady's maid."

David eyed him. "I think we need to be caught up here."

Marcus was about to explain when a thought occurred to him and he turned back to the children. "How did you get here?"

Isabelle answered. "They overheard Thomas' name and asked people on the street."

It was exactly the answer he had feared. He turned back to the others. "No time to explain. If Madeleine is the missing woman, and she was supposed to come here last night, then she's likely dead. Whoever killed her also killed her family to preserve the secret. They'll be looking for these children, which means we're no longer safe here."

Simon peered out the window, open only a hair. "How long do you think we have?"

"Not long. Whoever Lord François has hired is clearly good at their job if they were able to track her family down so quickly. If word spreads of two young children arriving here, a connection might be made."

"What do you propose?"

Marcus chewed his cheek for a moment. "They can't stay here, and for now, I don't believe there's any place in the city where they would be safe."

"The fortress?" suggested David.

"Normally, I would agree. However, with who's involved, I think it's best we keep the Order out of it for now."

"The farm?"

Marcus nodded. "That's exactly what I was thinking. Jeremy, take your horses to the Fortress. Exchange them for fresh ones plus two more, provisioned for the journey. Get provisions for three days for me and the sergeant and our horses, then bring the horses to the back alley."

"Yes, sir."

"And tell Sir Matthew that I will likely miss our scheduled meeting."

"Yes, sir."

"David, you go to Mrs. Thibault's and let Thomas know what has happened and that it's no longer safe for him to be here. I recommend he come with us. Before you go, get our horses from the livery and take them to the alleyway."

"Yes, sir."

"As soon as everyone is back, we'll head for the farm. Once we're clear of the city, Simon and I will remain behind to deal with this. When you arrive safely at the farm, send us a message."

"Yes, sir," replied David.

"Off with you. We have little time."

The two squires bolted out the front and Marcus turned to the next order of business. "Miss Isabelle, I need you to ready these children for the journey. Whatever it is you think they'll need. When the squires return, we'll be leaving very quickly."

"Yes, sir." She hesitated. "And what about you? There will only be two of you to deal with these murderers."

Marcus glanced at Simon, seething in the corner, his fists clenching and unclenching. "With the state my sergeant is in, two might be all we need."

Palais de la Cité
Paris, Kingdom of France

François fastened the final button on his shirt as his physician, Clymence, wrote some notes behind him at his desk.

"And you're certain?"

Clymence returned his pen to the inkwell and turned in his chair to face his patient. "I'm afraid so. With this new development, there can be no doubt. My hope that you might have months was an error. Now that you're coughing up blood, I suspect the deterioration will be rapid, and in days, at best several weeks, you will no longer be able to breathe."

François closed his eyes. He didn't fear death. He had been preparing for it for months now, though he did fear what would come next. An eternity of punishment for what he was responsible for did scare him, though he held out some faint hope that perhaps the good Lord would forgive him for what he had done, for none of it was out of malice, it was all to protect his family.

"I understand you had a healthy baby boy?"

François nodded, forcing a weak smile. "Yes. We were most fortunate."

Clymence eyed him. "Yes, most."

François looked away, avoiding eye contact, Clymence's tone suggesting he was aware something was amiss.

"The good Lord must have heard your prayers."

François grunted. "Yes, he must have."

"With a male heir, now your family is taken care of."

"Yes," said François curtly, determined to end the conversation before it became too uncomfortable. "Well, as there is nothing that can be done to help me, then this will be the last time we see each other, I suspect."

Clymence rose from his chair and extended his hand, staring François in the eyes. "It has been an honor, Lord François. I fear your final days on this earth will be quite unpleasant, quite painful. Should you require it, simply send word, and I'll send along something for the pain."

"I appreciate that, though perhaps a little suffering will do my soul some good."

Clymence eyed him. "May I make a suggestion, Lord François?"

François shifted uncomfortably, Clymence still grasping his hand. "Of course."

"Confession is good for the soul."

François inhaled sharply, his heart hammering. "Some sins can only be confessed to the Lord Himself."

Clymence regarded him then lowered his voice. "If you fear that your sins may become known, then remember, even a priest whose flock is the lowliest of society, can hear your confession without ever knowing who you are."

François' nostrils flared at the realization that Clymence was right, and he smiled slightly, shaking the man's hand again. "You are a wise one, my friend, and I shall miss your counsel."

He let go of the man's hand and swiftly left the

room, a room he would never see again. And as he passed through the hallways of the palace, he ignored everyone, quickly making his way to collect his horse, for he had to meet with Passe.

But before he did so, he had one last piece of physician's advice to follow.

Approaching the Enclos du Temple, Templar Fortress
Paris, Kingdom of France

Jeremy's chest swelled as the towering walls of the massive Templar fortress located in the heart of Paris came into view. He never tired of seeing it, as it always reminded him of just how powerful the order he had been a member of for most of his life indeed was. The Order was wealthy, extremely wealthy, though he knew little of these things. People like him, even the knights like Sir Marcus, had all taken vows of poverty. The Order took care of them, sheltered them, clothed them, fed them, all in exchange for their devotion.

With what the wealthy Order possessed, it meant those shelters, those clothes, those meals, were better than what most people enjoyed, and it did create jealousies, especially among the nobility who felt no one should possess wealth without a title. What many of them failed to acknowledge was that the knights *did* have titles. They *were* nobility. A commoner couldn't be a knight, yet these thousands had all taken their vows, most giving up all or substantial portions of their lands and wealth to the Order.

And he was proud to be a part of it.

He approached the gates with David's horse tethered to his own, his brown tunic with Maltese cross emblazoned on his chest, indicating his rank. The guards hailed him.

"What's your business here today, Squire?"

"I have a message for Sir Matthew from my master, Sir Marcus de Rancourt, and I need to provision four horses."

"You've been here before?"

Jeremy nodded. "Several times."

The guard indicated for the gates to be opened. "Then you'll know where to go. Welcome to the Fortress."

Jeremy bowed slightly in his saddle then headed inside. He came to a halt in front of the main building. A stableboy that he recognized as Quentin, who had helped them before, rushed over, grabbing the reins of his horse.

"Good day to you, Squire. It is good to see you again. What do you require?"

"Four fresh horses, all provisioned for a two-day ride, plus the provisions for a knight, sergeant, and their two horses, enough for three days."

"And when will you need this by?"

"Immediately."

"Understood."

Quentin took the horses and ran them around the corner toward the stables, shouting orders to other boys that did so much of the labor around here in exchange for a life that didn't involve living on the streets as orphans. Many, like himself, would become squires and perhaps, even one day, sergeants.

He stepped inside the building, his eyes adjusting to the reduced lighting. A sergeant sat at a table in the center of the large room. Jeremy hurried up to him and bowed. "I have an urgent message for Sir Matthew."

The sergeant glanced up at him, no doubt noting the color of his tunic. "One moment." He was writing something, his hands drawing the letters in a painfully slow manner. Jeremy's toe tapped with impatience.

"Can I just tell you the message and then leave? My master needs me urgently."

"One moment."

Jeremy spun on his heel in frustration, then spotted Sir Matthew walking with another knight at the far end of the room. Jeremy raised his hand. "Sir Matthew!" His voice echoed among the stone walls and marble floors. Sir Matthew glanced over then beckoned him with a wave of a hand, Jeremy having met the man before. He rushed over in as dignified a manner as he could manage, for this was the most senior Templar in the entire kingdom.

"What is it, Squire? Jeremy was it?"

Jeremy bowed deeply. "Yes, sir. You honor me by remembering my name."

Matthew smirked slightly. "Perhaps I remember it for whenever I see you, trouble is afoot."

Jeremy stared at the floor. "I'm sure I don't know what you mean, sir."

Matthew laughed. "Why are you here? Let me guess, something has happened and your master will be missing his appointment with me later today?"

"Yes, sir. An urgent matter has come up that he's dealing with. He fears it may take him several days to sort out, and sends his apologies."

"And this business, is it Templar business?"

Jeremy shook his head. "No, sir. He specifically said he doesn't want the Order involved lest it cause…difficulties, shall we say?"

"Difficulties? Interesting. So, this personal business is more important than his obligations to me and the

Order?"

Jeremy gulped, uncertain as to what to say. "I shouldn't say that, sir, however, it is a matter of life and death."

This appeared to pique Matthew's curiosity. "Life and death?"

"Yes, sir. At least five are dead already."

Matthew dismissed the other knight with a wave of his hand. "Tell me everything."

Outside the Durant Residence
Paris, Kingdom of France

Marcus led the way out of the alley, Tanya happily at his side, her tongue hanging out of her mouth, her tail wagging as Simon brought up the rear. David and Jeremy flanked the horses with Isabelle and Thomas, each carrying one of the children. Enzo was remaining behind, which suited Marcus just fine. Few would dare harm Thomas' household as long as the beast of a man might be inside.

The only advantage to leaving through the alleyway was that it had allowed them to prepare out of sight, rather than on the street for all to see. Anyone in the know, and he suspected that would be most of the neighborhood, would be fully aware of where they were coming from. He had debated hiding their identities as Templars, but decided against it. They didn't have the numbers to fight a large contingent. From what Enzo had explained, word would be put out to watch for the children, and a reward would likely be offered. Four normal men on horseback, protecting two people known to the neighborhood not to have children, might prove too tempting a target if the reward were large enough. But four Templars?

That was an entirely different thing.

They emerged onto the road, and as he expected, everyone took notice. There were some friendly waves as he and his men had done good in this neighborhood, and those aware of those deeds didn't fear him or his men. He smiled pleasantly, returning the waves, setting an easy pace as if there were no urgency to their journey.

"Sir, to your left," whispered David.

Marcus didn't turn his head, instead eying the direction his squire had indicated. Three young boys were huddled together, one of them pointing. The tallest, and he assumed the oldest, scurried away, and Marcus cursed. They had been recognized for who they were.

And their journey was about to get much more dangerous.

Gerart raced toward Mr. Passe's residence, his heart pounding with excitement. He couldn't be sure that what they had seen was definitely who they were searching for, but even if there were only a remote possibility, it had to be reported. One thousand *deniers* was too much of a reward to risk passing up on self-doubt, even if split three ways. He had no idea what that would amount to, but he was certain it was far more money than he had ever seen in his life.

It might even be enough to buy his way back into his family home.

A lump formed in his throat as he recalled the day his father kicked him out. It was two years ago, and he had snapped at his mother yet again for some petty reason. His father had grabbed him by the nape of the neck and tossed him out into the mud, telling him to never come back. Every day he'd spend a few minutes standing at the corner near his house, staring at the door, hoping for a glimpse of his mother or sisters.

Sometimes he'd be rewarded with a few precious moments. A few months ago, when his mother had stepped outside, he had lingered long enough for her to spot him. Tears had flowed down his cheeks at the joy on her face. She had rushed back in, appearing a moment later with his father. Gerart had ducked out of sight, then peered back for a moment. He could have sworn his father was disappointed to not see him. Had things changed? Had he been forgiven? It had been so long. Did they even care about him anymore? All he could say for certain was that he still cared for them, and would never dream of taking his mother for granted again.

He desperately wanted to return home. He couldn't stand the life he now had, though there was no denying it had improved since he began working for Passe. He and his two friends had become quite adept at lifting purses and other items of value that they would then bring to Passe. They would be rewarded with a small share of the take, but more importantly, they would be fed and given a roof to sleep under if their haul were especially good that day.

He had been raised a good Christian, and had attended church every Sunday for as long as he could remember. He was fully aware that everything he was now doing were sins against God. Yet he had no choice. He had to survive, and in Paris that meant becoming a thief. He had lost count of the number of nights he had cried himself to sleep, and there was little shame in it. Dozens of boys crammed together in a cold basement meant there were always at least several of them joining in. Most of them were miserable, those who weren't were truly twisted, eager to reach the age where they could join Passe's crew and become real criminals.

He feared that might be his future as well, but what

he had seen just minutes ago could change all that—Templars escorting two children. Two clean children. And all of them appeared terrified. Everyone was on the lookout for a woman with a cut face, and two young children, perhaps together, perhaps not. And though this didn't exactly match the description of the group they were looking for, it was simply too out of the ordinary to not be reported.

His parents had always said good things about Templars, though Passe and his men never had anything complimentary to say, which in his mind gave further credence to his parents' assessment of the Templar character. If these Templars were escorting children, children who appeared frightened for their lives, then they were doing a good deed, and what better deed than to save those whom a man like Passe was searching for?

It was a stretch, but if these were who Passe was seeking, and he were to receive his share of the reward, he could return home, present the deniers to his father, then beg his forgiveness and hope he'd be invited back into the home he yearned to rejoin.

He rounded the corner and spotted Passe's house just ahead. A smile spread, then he skidded to a halt, a frown replacing it. A pit formed in his stomach at a thought. If he passed on this information and Passe captured the children he was looking for, what would become of them? Would they be killed? Would he be responsible for their deaths? He shook his head. No. All he was doing was providing information. What Passe did with it wasn't his responsibility. He was just a child, a child who desperately wanted to go home, to return to his family. He needed that reward, no matter the consequences for someone else, for strangers.

He swallowed hard then marched toward Passe's home, his stomach a confused mess over the horrors of what he was about to do and the excitement of reuniting with his family. He closed his eyes, tears burning his eyelids at what might be his final, sinful act.

One by far the worst he had ever committed.

Madeleine peered out from her hiding place, weak and in agony. Her face was slashed open and her clothes were covered in blood. She was tired, weak, thirsty, and hungry. And she didn't know what to do or where to go. When she had escaped, she had rushed back to her sister's house to warn them. She couldn't care less what happened to her brother-in-law, but her sister, niece, and nephew didn't deserve to die for decisions she had made. But when she arrived, it was too late. She could hear the screams as untold things were done to her sister, and wept in the shadows as she waited for the men to leave.

When they finally did, she had sneaked inside, discovering the horrifying scene of her sister and brother-in-law, Grace defiled and gutted, Alain sliced from the belly to the chest. And the children were gone. She hadn't noticed the villains who had committed this atrocity carrying her niece and nephew, so she had to think they had escaped somehow. Louise was a bright girl of twelve, who just might have kept a level head and escaped with her brother the moment the attack began.

But where would they have gone? She had hidden in the nearby alleyway, struggling to stay awake in case she spotted them, but instead had passed out, waking hours later. The sun was shining and the streets were alive, which was exactly what she didn't want. Her only hope was to reach the Templars. She was now certain her brother-in-law had never spoken to them, so they weren't expecting her, but the logic that they would be the ones who could help her was still sound, and she could think of nowhere else to go.

She had covered the bloodstains on her clothes with mud, and twisted her head, facing her wound toward the ground, then hunched her shoulder, taking to the street with a makeshift cane that was merely a discarded piece of wood. By playing the decrepit old woman, perhaps diseased, no one would pay her any mind, and would most likely avoid her. It didn't take her long to reach Thomas' house. There were no horses out front, no signs of life, and her heart sank. Perhaps the Templars had already left. If that were the case, then she didn't dare approach the residence, for if she were recognized, it would put Thomas' life in danger.

She crouched in an alleyway down the street, just across from the livery she had reached last night before she was accosted. As she watched, she noticed there were men and children approaching everybody, asking them questions, and she had little doubt they were searching for her. She wept in despair, uncertain as to what to do. Her sister and brother-in-law were dead, but her niece and nephew might be out there somewhere, cold and alone, orphaned because of her. The only friends she had ever known besides Lady Denise had been raped and murdered, and now the Templars that might help her were nowhere to be found.

She had to find the children then somehow escape to another city where they might lose themselves. But how would she possibly do that? A woman with two children couldn't hope to walk that distance, and they couldn't afford to hire a carriage.

Horses whinnied and her heart leaped as a Templar Knight in full regalia emerged from an alleyway just past Thomas' house. He was accompanied by two squires, a sergeant, along with the largest dog she had ever seen, and she nearly cried out when she recognized Thomas, then did cry out when she saw he was holding Louise in front of him on the horse. Her eyes darted to the sixth horse in the procession. A young woman was on the back, strikingly beautiful, but she didn't recognize her. Yet that didn't matter. She was holding Monte. Tears flowed with the realization that not only were her sweet, brilliant niece and nephew alive, they had found the very help she was seeking.

She wasn't sure what to do. Should she reveal herself and pray that these men would help her, or would that just put the children at risk? But they were her family, and their parents were dead. Who would take care of them? She spotted three boys nearby, one of them pointing at the procession, another racing away, and her heart leaped into her throat. They had to be part of the group behind this. Children were used all the time as lookouts and messengers because they attracted little attention. Whoever they were, she had no doubt that their masters would be informed momentarily that her niece and nephew had been spotted with Templars.

She made a decision that she prayed didn't harm the children.

"Louise! Monte!" She rushed from her hiding place, waving her hand. The knight leading the procession turned his head but kept everyone moving forward, a hand reaching for the hilt of his sword. The squire nearest her swiftly retrieved his bow and had an arrow fitted and aimed at her in quick fashion. She kept on. He was a Templar and wouldn't loose on an unarmed woman. "Louise! Monte! It's Aunt Madeleine!"

Louise, terror in her eyes, suddenly brightened. "Auntie!" she cried. Monte, who had been staring straight ahead, trembling, spun his head toward her, a smile spreading as he too cried out for her. Thomas stared at her, recognition on his face as his jaw dropped, evidently not realizing he knew the family the children belonged to.

"Madeleine?"

When she stared up at him, he gasped in horror and she placed a hand over her wound. "Yes, Thomas, it's me! I need your help!"

The knight at the head of the procession turned in his saddle, pointing at the squire with the bow and arrow still aimed at her. "We don't have any time for this. Jeremy, put her on your horse." Jeremy slung his bow and reached out an arm. Madeleine took it and was swung onto the rear of the horse, and within moments, they were on their way again, though this time at a quicker pace.

She smiled at Louise directly beside her with Thomas. "I'm so happy you're all right."

"Mother and Father are dead," said the girl before she wailed.

The knight turned. "Please try to keep her quiet. We're drawing too much attention as it is. Everybody just keep your eyes open for anything. Should we be separated, head for the Templar Fortress and use my name to get in."

Madeleine eyed him. "What is your name?"

"Sir Marcus de Rancourt, ma'am." He pointed to her right. "Watch for anything unusual, and don't be afraid to speak up."

"Yes, sir." She redirected her eyes, Louise already down to a whimper. Madeleine's pulse pounded in her ears as she finally noticed just how on edge everyone was. There was no way her niece and nephew could know what was going on, which meant these people already did know. They were Templars, and she never thought them to be scared of anything, yet they were still just men, not legend. If they were on edge, then they must be fully aware somehow of what was happening, and it meant she and the children weren't safe at all.

Passe Residence
Paris, Kingdom of France

Gerart rushed into Passe's house, running headlong into Bertaut.

"What's got you in such a hurry, boy?"

"I might have found them!"

Bertaut's eyes narrowed. "Found who?"

"The children. I just saw two clean kids, like you said to watch for, but they were with Templars. Templars don't have children, do they?"

Bertaut appeared excited. "No, they don't. Who else was with them?"

"A man and a woman, each with one of the children on their horses."

Bertaut frowned. "And why wouldn't you think the children belong to them?"

"Because they're too young, and the children are too old."

"Where?"

"Not far. My friends are following them. We can catch them if we hurry."

"How many Templars?"

"Four."

"Four knights?"

Gerart shrugged. "I have no idea. How can you tell?"

"The color of their tunics."

He squinted as he struggled to remember. "One white, one black, two brown."

Bertaut smiled slightly. "That will be no problem. Up the stairs with you."

Gerart grinned and rushed up the steps, Bertaut on his heels, and they were soon in Passe's empty office. Gerart's eyes bulged at the sight of a bejeweled dagger hanging on the wall behind the boss' desk, and it had him wondering how many deniers it might be worth.

Bertaut cursed and closed the door. "Forget what you saw."

Gerart gulped. "Yes, sir."

Bertaut stepped over to the next set of stairs leading to the top floor.

"Boss! We may have found the children!"

Strange sounds Gerart hadn't noticed until now suddenly ceased. Floorboards creaked overhead and a door opened.

"What did you say?"

"Gerart and his friends may have found the two children. They're with a group of four Templars. A knight, a sergeant, and two squires."

"When did they last see them?"

Bertaut smacked Gerart on the shoulder and he stepped forward. "Only just now, sir. As soon as we spotted them, I ran here. My friends will follow. If we hurry, we can catch them for sure."

"Get every man you can on a horse. Double them up if you have to. I want to be out of here in five minutes."

"Yes, sir."

Gerart held out his hand. "What about my reward?"

"What did he say?" shouted Passe from above.

"He wants to know about his reward, sir."

There was a laugh. "Tell the boy he'll get it when we have the children. For now, tell him to wait outside so he can lead us to where he saw them."

Bertaut swatted him again on the shoulder. "You heard the man."

Gerart jumped with excitement. "Yes, sir!" He darted down the stairs and sat on the step in front of the residence as orders were barked inside. Men charged past him, heading toward the stables just down the road, a man on the rooftop shouting instructions in code, the tiny voices of people like him relaying the message, and within moments, the entire neighborhood was aware that something was afoot.

But most of it was lost on him, including the sinful deed he had just done.

For now, all of his thoughts were consumed with just what one-thousand deniers looked like, and how it would bring him back to his family.

Leaving the Durant Residence
Paris, Kingdom of France

"Sir, we're being followed. Two children on our left."

Marcus kept pressing forward, the hoofbeats of the six horses clearing the crowds ahead. He spotted the two children behind them, sprinting to keep up. Two well-placed arrows would end the pursuit and ensure their escape, however he would never give such an order. These children were victims, taken advantage of by men like Passe and even women like Thibault. They were doing what they needed to survive. They were mostly orphans, their parents dead, or from families who couldn't afford them, or from families they had escaped from. If they had come from a stable home, the vast majority would have grown into decent God-fearing adults rather than turning to a life of crime.

The Templars helped where they could by employing stableboys and providing them with food and shelter, but the numbers were simply too great. Everywhere one looked on the streets of Paris, one could find a child begging, sobbing, or stealing. They were desperate, and he swore the two young souls he now protected wouldn't suffer such a fate.

Yet they had to escape.

The children needn't keep up for long before it would be too late. The first child they had seen run away would have already revealed their position, presumably to Passe. He would have immediately mobilized any men he had on hand, and if it were his men that had committed the murders outside of Paris, then they obviously had some horses available. They would be galloping through the streets, unconcerned with those who might get in the way, and unburdened by children and inexperienced riders.

He glanced back and his eyes narrowed at the two boys chasing them. They weren't the same boys as a few minutes ago. That's when he realized what was happening. There were children throughout the area, and when the pursuers would encounter their associates, they would switch, giving a fresh set of legs for the chase and leaving behind the tired legs to point their masters in the right direction. There was no way he could get them out of the city in time without breaking the chain.

And that was something he wasn't willing to do.

"We've got company!" shouted Simon from the rear.

Marcus continued forward, twisting in his saddle. He cursed at the sight of several men on horseback. "David, see what you can do!"

"Yes, sir!" David fell back slightly, his bow and arrow already out.

Marcus returned his attention to the road in front of them. The distinctive twang of the bow's string snapping setting him at ease slightly as no one could match David's skills, and their pursuers wouldn't risk getting too close, lest they fall victim to one of his squire's arrows. He noticed a horseman to their left emerging from an intersecting street. The man drew a sword but Marcus didn't slow, instead drawing his own and tossing the blade in the air, catching it with his left hand. He shifted slightly in his saddle, the reins no longer gripped, his well-trained beast responding by drifting them closer to his target. The man's eyes bulged at what was about to happen. He gripped his sword in both hands, holding it out in front of him as if it were a javelin, though one far too short to be effective. Marcus swung his blade, his injured shoulder still feeling the effects from last year, making its disapproval known. As he swung low then upward, he caught the outside of the man's blade, his grip broken instantly as the two weapons collided. Marcus' blade continued upward, slicing through the man's right arm as they charged by, leaving his opponent out of the battle. He might survive if he received medical attention soon, but Marcus didn't care.

The man worked for those who would traffic in children.

Two more horsemen appeared ahead and Marcus cursed. They were being outflanked. He glanced back to see David still covering their rear. The horsemen behind them, now numbering at least half a dozen, keeping their distance. Archers were their best defense at the moment, and one of them couldn't join the fight because he had the woman riding with him.

"Jeremy!" He beckoned him forward with a wave of his hand. Jeremy urged his horse ahead and they were soon at each others' side. Marcus reached out to the woman. "Get on my horse!" he ordered. Her eyes bulged, but to her credit, she didn't hesitate. She pushed up on Jeremy's shoulders, balancing on the back of the saddle, then grabbed Marcus' arm with her opposing hand and leaped across, wrapping both arms around Marcus' neck as she settled in.

"Cover the front!" ordered Marcus, and Jeremy surged ahead, his bow and arrow now free to cover them in all directions. "Take out anyone who draws a sword!" An arrow loosed and a rider ahead that Marcus hadn't noticed yet cried out, falling from his saddle as they charged forward, the streets clearing rapidly as the thunder of a dozen galloping beasts was accompanied by the shouts and screams of battle and pain.

They were near the outskirts now, and soon would be on the only road to home. If they could just reach it, there would be no more surprises from ahead, but it would also mean their only defense would be their archers, who would soon be out of arrows.

"That's Passe behind us!" yelled Thomas.

Marcus glanced behind him at the half-dozen riders following them. David was no longer engaging, merely holding them at bay with a readied arrow, only three left in his quiver. "Which one?"

"The short one in the fine clothes!"

Marcus picked him out, burning his features into his memory for when justice would be delivered. They were almost at the city's edge to the lone road that would lead them to their home, several hours ride from here. But they couldn't keep this pace. The horses would give out soon enough, though so should their pursuers', and he was confident their Templar-supplied horses were of sturdier stock. Which was why that wasn't his primary concern.

It was the road ahead.

If it were crowded, they would be overtaken quickly and they might be overwhelmed, depending on the numbers. This plan of action had failed, and he could see only one option.

"Jeremy! We have to head for the Fortress!"

Jeremy loosed another arrow, another target taken

down. The squire glanced over his shoulder at his master and shook his head. "No, sir! We must keep going!"

Marcus glared at his squire. It wasn't like him to question an order, especially in the heat of battle. The houses were thinning now as they passed through the outskirts of the mass of humanity that called Paris home. Once they were on the road, they were committed for several miles before there was another that intersected their path, giving them three options, none of which were good. If they didn't turn now, they were stuck, but if they did, they could reach the fortress in less than a quarter-hour.

The decision had to be made.

And he had already made it.

"Next road, we turn right! That's an order!"

Jeremy drew his final arrow, fitting it in place. As he continued to charge forward, he pulled back on the string but held tight, the man it was intended for tipping over the side of his horse, using it as a shield. As they charged past, Marcus could see the green ahead, a color missing in the slums, and their last chance to turn was rapidly approaching.

Jeremy looked over his shoulder, showing no signs of slowing to make the turn. "We must continue forward!"

For the first time in years, Marcus felt genuine anger toward his squire. "You have your orders, Squire!"

"Yes, sir, I do, and I'm following them!" Jeremy leaned forward in his saddle, charging past the final turn to safety. Marcus could leave his trusted man to his own devices and certain death, or follow him. Something was going on. This was entirely out of character for

Jeremy. What was it he had said when told to follow his orders?

I'm following them.

Marcus' heart hammered as he realized what must be going on, and he turned to the others. "Follow Jeremy!"

Simon's eyes widened slightly, though he didn't question the order. They charged past their final chance at reaching the Fortress where hundreds of their fellow Templars were stationed, where not even the King could touch them.

He just prayed he hadn't sealed their fate.

A House of God
Paris, Kingdom of France

To say the church was humble would be an understatement. François had rid himself of anything that could identify him in preparation for the meeting with Passe, and it would serve him well here. The slums were disgusting, filthy, wretched, yet despite its decrepit state, this was still a house of God, and the priest who sat on the other side of the confessional was as Christian as any, and likely more pious than François' own priest who lived far more comfortable a life than this poor soul. Confession to a priest like this, he had no doubt, would carry far more weight than any made to a man who catered to the whims of the rich.

He had been reluctant at first to say anything, though with the encouragement of this priest, a man he had never seen before and whom he would never see again, he finally spoke, and it was the truth, the entire truth.

Except for his name.

The priest had sat silently at first, occasionally asking a question as the story became more detailed. François could hear a tinge of horror in the man's voice when the tale of the murder of the staff was related. But it wasn't until he revealed that the hunt was still on for Madeleine that the priest expressed righteous indignation.

"You're telling me, my son, that you've come here to confess your sins, yet there's a woman out there whose life is in danger?"

"Yes, Father."

"And you don't see a problem with that?"

François sighed, his shoulders slumping. "Yes, Father, I do, but I don't see how to divert from the path I'm now on. So many sins have been committed, so much blood spilled, that if I stop now, all of that will have been for nothing. But once the secret is preserved, the little boy will be raised as my son, my daughters' lives will be saved from the horrors of impoverished nobility, and so will my wife's."

"So, you justify the murder of one more innocent woman because you want your wife and daughters to have a comfortable life. Why can't you provide that to them?"

"I'm dying. I have only weeks, perhaps days, to live." He gasped at saying it aloud for the first time, and bit on a knuckle to maintain control. "I need to secure their futures before I die and my title and fortune are passed to my brother, whom I haven't spoken to in over a decade, and who despises me."

"I see," said the priest. "Your desperate situation drove you to take desperate action. Yet none of it is an excuse for kidnapping and murder."

"I realize that now, Father. If I had known before I began how I would feel today, I never would have done what I did. I would have found another way. It was only supposed to be a kidnapping. It never occurred to me about the secret needing to be kept. In retrospect, it would have been better to use legitimate channels and buy a baby from a couple willing to give him up and planned around that, but in my panic, I made foolish decisions."

"And you continue to make them."

"Yes, I do."

"Then why are you here now, confessing your sins?"

"I don't want to burn in Hell for eternity for what I have done. I'm not a bad man, I never have been. I treat my family, friends, and staff well. I always advocate on behalf of the poor and give generously every Sunday at church. I was a good man until my illness was revealed to me and I set upon this desperate course where I could no longer trust that time would take care of my daughters through their own marriages, and they would subsequently tend to their mother after I died years from now. I was a good man, and while I deserve punishment, and was willing to face that for eternity, I was hoping that by confessing my sins, when I die in the coming days, the good Lord might take it upon Himself to eventually forgive me for what I've done, realizing that the actions over two weeks, where no malice was intended, no pleasure was taken, shouldn't negate a lifetime of service."

The priest sat silently on the other side of the confessional, then finally spoke. "You do understand how confession works, do you not?"

François squinted. "I always thought I did."

"In order to forgive you for your sins, I must believe that not only do you regret them, but that you'll never commit them again."

"I can assure you, Father, even if I were to live a thousand years, I would never repeat the sins of the past few days."

"I believe you, and I am prepared to forgive you for everything you've committed up to this point, and your penance will occupy much of your remaining days. However, there is one sin that I cannot forgive you for."

François' relief was short-lived. "And what is that, Father?"

"I cannot forgive you for the sins you have yet to commit. If the woman your people now pursue comes to any harm, no priest anywhere, that you are honest with, will forgive you."

François gulped. "But what if I can't stop them?"

"I suggest you don't let that be a possibility, otherwise the eternal damnation you fear so much will be unavoidable."

Lord François de Montglat Estate
Paris, Kingdom of France

Helene knocked gently on her mother's door. "Mother, it's me. May I come in?"

"Yes."

She opened the door and stepped inside. The new lady's maid, Blanche, was tending to her mother's hair in preparation for dinner.

"What is it, dear?"

"I need to speak with you."

"Go ahead."

Helene glanced at Blanche. If it were Madeleine, she wouldn't hesitate. She had known Madeleine her entire life and trusted her like family. While she knew this woman, it had only been for a few years, and never in a situation where family confidences were shared.

"When you hear what I wish to speak to you of, you may not feel the same way."

Her mother sighed then flicked her wrist. "Give us a few minutes, would you?"

"Of course, milady." Blanche bowed then left the room, closing the door behind her.

Her mother turned to face her. "Now, what is it, my child, that would have you leaving your mother's hair in such a state?"

Helene's heart pounded with fear and excitement. She sat on the edge of the bed, wringing her hands in her lap. "I wish to speak to you of someone."

Her mother's eyebrows climbed slightly. "Oh,

some*one*, not some*thing*?"

Helene's cheeks flushed. "Yes, some*one*."

Her mother smirked. "Some man?"

Helene's cheeks were now on fire, but a smile spread at the thought of that man. "Yes."

"And who, pray tell, is this man that has caught your eye?"

She lifted her gaze and stared at her mother. "Oh, Mother, it's so much more than my eye he's caught! He owns my heart! It came as a shock even to me, but when I saw him today, I realized that every time I've seen him over the past several years, he's excited me for days, if not weeks on end. I've always thought of it as a little girl's infatuation, but today when I saw him, I knew he was the one. And when we spoke, he confirmed to me that he has feelings as well. Oh, Mother, I so hope you would give your approval. If you approve, then I know Father will."

Her mother laughed. "I can hardly think we'd object unless he's the most vile of creatures. But who could you be speaking of? The only person I'm aware of who visited here today is…" Her eyes shot wide and her jaw dropped. "Not Sir Denys!"

Helene's chest tightened at the reaction. It was the reaction she had feared. She bowed her head, avoiding eye contact. "Yes, Mother. It's Sir Denys."

Her mother appeared to be at a loss for words, and Helene had to take advantage. She leaned forward, staring into her mother's eyes. "Mother, please, if you had heard his words today, they were so eloquent, so in earnest. He says he's a changed man. He's sworn to become a better person to regain the respect of the Court and his family, and to start a family of his own.

He really isn't a bad person."

Her mother sucked in a deep breath. "You don't know of what you speak. He is not a man of questionable character. He's a man of *no* character!"

"But can't a man change? If a good man can become bad, then can't a bad man become good?"

Her mother glared at her. "What do you mean by that?"

Helene was taken aback at the snapped question. "What do I mean by what?"

"That a good man can become bad. Why did you say that?"

Helene stared at her mother wide-eyed. "I don't know. I was just thinking that not all bad men were always bad. Was Judas always evil? Or did something twist him into what he became? And I've heard the stories told of Sir Denys, and he's certainly not an evil man. It's not like he's ever hurt anybody or killed anybody. Surely, a man who enjoyed the sins available to him a little too much in his youth doesn't deserve to be condemned his entire life. He genuinely wants to make a change for the better."

Her mother appeared to relax slightly, and Helene pressed on. "Please, Mother, give him your blessing. I promise that should he prove to not be a man of his word, I will end it. You know I would do nothing to damage the reputation of this family. He comes from a good family, and if he reforms himself, no shame would be brought to us, for I'm certain his past sins would be forgiven. He only needs to be given a chance. Please, Mother, tell me you'll speak to Father on Sir Denys' behalf."

Her mother pursed her lips, her head slowly

shaking. "Very well," she finally said. "I will speak to your father and see what he has to say about it, as I'm certain he has no idea Sir Denys will be calling upon him for permission to court his daughter."

Helene giggled. "Oh, to see Father's face when he's asked!"

Her mother laughed. "Can you imagine?"

"When it happens, I shall endeavor to be on the other side of the door."

Her mother's face slackened slightly. "Please tell me you don't do that."

Helene was taken aback. "Don't do what?"

"Listen at our door."

Her mouth widened in horror. "I would never dream of doing such a thing! I merely said it in jest!"

Her mother regarded her for a moment. "Very well." She wagged a finger. "But you must never listen at a door, especially the door of your parents' bedchambers or your father's office. Things are discussed that are not for the ears of children."

She frowned at her mother. "I'm not a child. We've just been discussing the man I hope to marry."

Her mother reached out and patted her hand. "You know what I mean."

Helene sighed. "Yes, I do, Mother. But you'll speak to Father?"

"I shall."

"How do you think he'll react?"

Her mother shrugged. "I can think of several possibilities. He'll reluctantly agree to allow it, he'll outright refuse it, or he'll turn Sir Denys into a eunuch."

Helene's eyes narrowed in confusion then shot wide

as she finally realized what her mother meant. She blushed and giggled. "Then I hope for Sir Denys' sake it's one of the first two options."

Her mother laughed. "I'm sure he hopes so as well."

Leaving Paris, Kingdom of France

Jeremy charged forward, his heart pounding, not in fear of the situation, but at the anger he had heard directed toward him by Sir Marcus. He had disobeyed a direct order, and wasn't certain why his master had agreed to continue, though it had to be the trust built over their many years together. The path they were committed to now was a dangerous one, and as the road slowly narrowed, barely wider than the wheels of a carriage would require, they had little hope of escape now that they were hemmed in by thick brush on either side. He glanced back to see the others directly behind them, though they were going slower than if it were just the four of them. Thomas and Isabelle, each holding a child, were slowing them down, and even if they weren't encumbered, the two, especially Thomas, weren't experienced riders.

Yet it shouldn't be long.

In fact, it should be any moment now where the dozen riders behind them, many carrying a second man, would be in for a shock. He redirected his eyes forward, his horse, well aware of her duty, charging ahead, sensing the tension of her master. Then he finally spotted what he'd been waiting for, and a smile spread at the promise kept.

Scores of Templar knights and sergeants, and a small army of squires to support them, were spread out ahead on either side of the road, their colors proudly on display. He charged toward them, not slowing. He spotted Sir Matthew on his horse at the edge of the road, another formidable knight on the opposite side. Jeremy raced between them, maintaining his speed for several moments until he was certain the rest had made it through the formation of warrior monks. He pulled up on the reins, bringing his beast to a halt, then rose in his saddle as the others came to rest near him.

The way behind them filled with Templars and their pursuers came to a halt in a mass of confusion as they attempted to turn a dozen large animals around on the narrow road. Not a single sword was drawn nor a bow readied, the mere presence of the formidable Templar force enough to put the fear of God into these criminals, and within moments, they were beating a hasty retreat back toward Paris.

Marcus helped the mysterious woman to the ground and she rushed over to the children. He approached Jeremy with a smirk and bent over to pat a panting Tanya. "You knew about this, didn't you?"

Matthew stepped over. "Don't be angry at your squire, Sir Marcus. It was my orders that he was following."

"And your orders included lying to me?"

Jeremy's jaw dropped. "I never once lied to you, sir!"

Marcus regarded him. "Lie of omission then?"

Jeremy shrugged. "I have no idea what that means."

Marcus laughed. "Don't play the fool I know you not to be."

Jeremy stared at the muddy ground. "Yes, sir."

Matthew chuckled and slapped Marcus on the shoulder. "Don't be so hard on the man. After all, he might have just saved your life."

Marcus stared at the retreating horde. "It was only

twenty against four. I still think we would have prevailed."

Matthew laughed. "I have no doubt, Sir Marcus, I have no doubt. When your squire came to see me to deliver your message that you'd be missing our meeting, I insisted he tell me everything. I decided it was best to bring a contingent out, merely on an exercise, mind you, in the event you ran into trouble. If you had escaped Paris unnoticed, it would have merely been a pleasant chance encounter. But if you were in trouble, like you evidently were, we could intervene as you were Templars under attack. Either way, the Templar Order isn't involved in this situation in which you've become entangled."

Marcus nodded. "It is fortunate then, that you questioned my squire."

Simon grunted. "I'm surprised he was able to keep the secret. Normally, when he knows something, he has a shit-eating grin on his face until he finally reveals all."

"That doesn't sound like me," mumbled Jeremy.

David smacked him on the back. "Oh, that's so you! How *did* you keep the secret?"

"I never had a chance to tell anyone! As soon as I arrived with the horses, we left."

Matthew motioned for one of the squires to bring over his horse. "We should head for the Fortress now. I don't think it's wise for you to continue to your farm in case they know of its existence."

Marcus agreed. "We'll regroup at the Fortress, then determine what to do next. But I must insist on one thing, Sir Matthew."

Matthew cocked an eyebrow. "And that is?"

"That the Order remains neutral in this."

"On that, Sir Marcus, I wholeheartedly agree."

Passe Residence
Paris, Kingdom of France

Passe's fists were clenched on the entire ride back to their home base. They had been defeated without a sword drawn. He punched the wall, splintering the wood as he climbed the stairs to his office, Bertaut on his heels. "We need archers."

"Sir?"

"You heard me. All we have are men with swords and daggers and fists. We need archers. If we had archers, we could have taken them out before they even reached the outskirts. They never would have reached their friends. How many of our men did they take out with their archers?"

Bertaut opened his mouth as if to answer, but Passe cut him off with a shake of his fist.

"It was a rhetorical question."

Bertaut's eyes narrowed, the man's mouth opening again.

Passe growled. "Don't you dare ask me what that means."

"Sorry, boss. Umm, what do we do now? If the Templars are protecting them, I don't see what we can do."

Passe stepped onto the platform holding his desk, then collapsed in his chair. He stared at the dagger hanging on the wall. He had hoped to have good news for Lord François, but now he had the worst possible—he had confirmation that the woman was alive, and that she was protected by the only people that couldn't be touched in the entire kingdom. He chewed his cheek for a moment as he thought about the situation. Those he was after were no doubt within the walls of the Fortress by now, or if they weren't, they soon would be. There was no way to attack that column even if they hadn't arrived yet. There were simply too many.

It was an overwhelming force, and there was no way they were there by coincidence. This had been planned, which meant the Templars had become involved, and that was never a good thing. Those their client wanted dead would be protected within the walls of the fortress, untouchable, until they chose to leave, perhaps in days or weeks.

A smile crept up his cheek as he realized he was wrong.

Bertaut picked up on the change of mood. "What is it, boss? Have you thought of something?"

Passe now sported a full smile. He stabbed a finger toward his man. "What are Templars?"

Bertaut folded his arms. "I'm not sure I should be answering any questions. They may be rhetor…what did you call it?"

"Rhetorical. And yes, keep your mouth shut and just listen. Templars are monks, sworn to celibacy. They don't let women sleep within their walls. They have a nunnery nearby. I have little doubt they'll be moving those we're after before nightfall."

"But they'll do it under guard, won't they?"

"I have no doubt they will, but there's another thing that Templars are."

Bertaut remained silent.

"They're arrogant."

"What does that mean, boss?"

Passe stared at him incredulously. "You don't know what arrogant means?"

"Of course I know what arrogant means. What I mean is, what does that *mean*? If they're arrogant, how does that help us?"

Passe was relieved that one of his most trusted men wasn't a complete idiot. "It means that they will be overconfident. They'll think there's no way we'd risk attacking them en route. I think they'll transfer them to the nunnery at dusk with a much smaller contingent, ten, maybe twenty at best. That will be our only chance to get them. Once they reach the nunnery and are within its walls, they'll be untouchable. It's too well-guarded."

Bertaut stared at him. It was clear the man desperately wanted to say something. Passe waved his hand. "Out with it."

Bertaut's eyes darted around the room, avoiding eye contact. "Well, sir, it's just that we got our asses kicked today. Like you said, we need archers, and we don't have them. I'm sure I could probably get some bows and arrows, but you and I both know that if you've never shot one, especially in battle, it's pointless."

Passe nodded. "I agree. We're going to need help."

"From whom?"

"From others of like mind."

Bertaut's eyebrows shot up his forehead. "Won't that be expensive?"

"We'll split the fee with any who will join us. This is no longer about profit, this is about reputation." He clenched an iron fist. "And nobody makes me look weak."

Enclos du Temple, Templar Fortress
Paris, Kingdom of France

Madeleine sat in a large chair, her niece and nephew in her lap, both sound asleep, exhausted from their terrifying adventure. The Templars were in another room with a man named Sir Matthew, whom she presumed was in charge, based upon the deference shown the man. Thomas sat nearby with the young blonde woman at his side, holding his hand, and the massive dog lay in front of the fire. Food and drink were brought in, then they were left alone again. The children stirred at the door closing, their faces lighting up at the meal. She motioned with her chin toward the table and they eagerly scrambled out of her lap, assaulting what was on offer.

"Do you want anything?" the young woman asked Thomas.

"I'm not really very hungry, but I suppose I should eat something."

He rose to get some food but the woman waved him off. "You sit. I'll get it."

Madeleine stared at Thomas. The last time she had seen him, he was still a boy, at least in her eyes. Now he was a young man who hadn't panicked during their ordeal, who had taken in children he didn't even know, who had risked his life because it was the right thing to do.

"It's good to see you again, Thomas."

He shook his head. "I still can't believe it's you. You were the person I least expected to see today of all days." He gestured at the children. "And to find out that they were your niece and nephew?" He shrugged. "I just don't know what to say to that."

"I say God had a plan, perhaps one laid out long ago when our families became friends, and I would look after you so both your mother and father could work. And He certainly had a plan when He put you in the path of those Templars. It saved us all today." She nodded toward the woman. "Now, are you going to introduce me to this young lady?"

Thomas flushed, a mix of embarrassment and pride. "Madeleine Rabot, may I introduce my fiancée, Isabelle Leblanc."

Isabelle executed an awkward curtsy. "Ma'am."

Madeleine beamed at them both. "Fiancée! I'm so proud of you, Thomas. You've turned into a fine young man. Your mother would be so proud, as would your father."

"Thank you."

"I was sorry to hear about what happened to your father last year. I only just found out last night, otherwise I would have sent my condolences."

Thomas' face clouded over, but he said nothing as Isabelle handed him something to eat. He took a bite of the bread, chewing slowly.

"And you, Miss Isabelle, how did you meet young Thomas?"

"Oh, it's a wonderful story!" She set her own food aside and leaned forward. "I—"

The door opened and Sir Marcus entered with his entourage, ending the conversation. The children scurried back into her arms, the figure the man cut imposing, though she sensed it was his sergeant they feared most.

Marcus nodded toward the bandage on her face. "I see they've treated you."

"Yes, sir. They said I'll have a nasty scar, but as long as it doesn't get infected, I should live."

"Good. Then let's make certain that it doesn't."

"Yes, sir."

"I've discussed it with Sir Matthew, and he's agreed that we can provide you all with temporary sanctuary until the situation is resolved. Unfortunately, the Templar Order cannot become involved officially, as this deals with a member of the King's Court, and the relationship between the Order and King Philip is tense at the moment. Especially when it comes to me."

Madeleine's eyes narrowed. "To you?"

The sergeant grunted. "Sir Marcus has put His Highness in his place a couple of times over the past year." Marcus held up a hand, cutting off what no doubt would have been a fascinating story or two.

Madeleine regarded the knight. "What was the original plan? You were leaving the city, if I'm not mistaken."

"We were heading to my farm."

Her eyes shot wide. "A Templar Knight has a farm?"

"It's a long story that I'll let Thomas and Isabelle fill you in on at some point, but for now, that plan is on hold until we can resolve this situation. While we may be able to sneak you out of the city and to the farm, we don't know if they're aware of its existence. If anyone recognized Thomas, and we have to assume somebody did, then we could be attacked there without the protection of the Order. For now, we're going to transfer you all to the nearby nunnery. It's a secure location and guarded by Templars. We'll increase the guard temporarily until we resolve this matter."

Isabelle asked the question begging to be answered. "But how are you going to resolve it?"

Marcus looked at her. "I intend to pay a visit to Lord François and put an end to this once and for all."

Courtyard of the Enclos du Temple, Templar Fortress
Paris, Kingdom of France

Marcus grunted, his left shoulder twinging from the weight of the shield David had just handed him. It was the first time he had carried all the accouterments of war since he had left the Holy Lands. The distance they had to travel was short, only several miles, but scouts had been sent out ahead through a secret exit, and the reports indicated suspicious activity along the route, including men on rooftops and horses.

The Templars' own intelligence network knew about Passe and others within the city involved in questionable activities. The Order always kept tabs on persons of concern among the populations that shared the locations they were stationed in. In the briefing he had received from one of their intelligence officers, he and Sir Matthew had been assured that Passe could field no more than two dozen men, and in their initial escape attempt, he had removed one from the field of battle, and David and Jeremy had seriously wounded or killed at least another half-dozen. It should mean that Passe could only field perhaps a dozen men now, though the scouting reports suggested far more.

"Have they been known to cooperate?" he had asked the intelligence officer.

"On occasion, sir, when their interests overlap."

"And would their interests overlap here?"

"They could. We are not very popular among the criminal element, so an opportunity to strike at us might be temptation enough, though I don't believe the casualties they would inevitably suffer would be worth it. Most likely, there's some sort of monetary incentive. You said this nobleman is quite wealthy. Without knowing his name, I can't confirm how wealthy he may be, but if he is, a man like Passe would charge him an exorbitant sum for the activities he's partaken in these past several days, especially if the nobleman has no experience in these matters and wouldn't know what the going rate should be."

Marcus shuddered at the memory. To think there was actually a going rate for kidnapping a newborn child, for murdering innocent women and children was heartbreaking. And it was the problem these women and children posed that had resulted in the activity around him. Women weren't allowed within the Fortress walls after dark, though exceptions could be made. Due to the current circumstances, Matthew had been willing to make that exception, but Marcus had recommended against it, as they had to limit the Order's involvement.

He was confident they could reach the nunnery. He glanced over his shoulder at the source of that confidence, and witnessing it in person left him with little doubt he was right. While they would no doubt fall under attack, the women and children would reach safety, for there was no penetrating the war wagon behind them, drawn by four horses, all armored, controlled by two coachmen, armored and enclosed, hauling the heavy wooden box that no arrow could penetrate.

Not to mention the fact it was locked from the inside and guarded by Simon himself.

Once they passed through the gates, they could be

attacked at any moment, and this time, he expected them to be better prepared. If they had men on the rooftops, it meant they had archers, something their enemy lacked during their first encounter.

Sir Matthew strode up to him, extending a hand. "Good luck, Sir Marcus. When you safely reach your destination, have a messenger sent. And shouldn't you…" The man hesitated and Marcus saved him.

"Should I and my men fall this day in battle, all I ask is that those at my farm be taken care of."

Matthew squeezed Marcus' hand harder. "You have my word."

And that was all Marcus needed to hear. Should he die this day, his family and the others would be taken care of by the Order he had dedicated himself to so many years ago. He let go of Matthew's hand and raised a fist in the air, everyone falling silent.

"Everyone knows their job. No matter what we face, that carriage gets to its destination. We may be outnumbered, but we're Templars, and no petty criminal will cause us to fail!" He smacked his armored chest with his closed fist, the others doing the same before he raised his arm and dropped it toward the gates. The massive doors swung aside and Marcus led the procession of half a dozen knights and their sergeants, plus a dozen squires, all trained as archers, including David and Jeremy.

As he cleared the gates and turned onto the road, he charged ahead with three of the knights, clearing a path, though finding few people. It was dusk, so most would either be at home or heading there, yet it was more than that. As they rushed ahead, he tensed, for there were too many eyes in the windows, as if the entire neighborhood were aware something was about to happen.

He slowed slightly.

"We're being watched," said the knight to his right.

Marcus agreed. "It would appear everyone knows we're coming, and the residents are all in hiding."

"Should we turn back?"

Marcus shook his head. "No. It means the road ahead will be clear, and anyone that moves is the enemy. All they've done is made our job easier."

"From your lips to God's ears, my friend."

Marcus laughed. "Let's hope He's listening. With Him on our side, we cannot fail."

Outside the Durant Residence
Paris, Kingdom of France

Denys leaned forward in his saddle, frowning, as one of his men once again rapped on the door of young Thomas Durant's residence. The man shook his head. "I'm sorry, sir. It would appear no one is home."

Denys cursed at having missed the Templars, then a thought struck him that had him concerned. "Force the door."

"Sir?"

"I said, force the door. We need to make sure they're not inside, dead."

The man stepped back, about to execute his order, when a deep voice resonated behind them. "What goes on here?"

Denys spun in his saddle to see a lumbering beast of a man that he knew to be Mrs. Thibault's enforcer. He couldn't remember the man's name, but the anger on the twisted face that approached already had his marshal and guards drawing their swords. Denys held out a hand, calling them off. "I am Sir Denys de Montfort. I am a friend of Sir Marcus de Rancourt. I am here out of concern for Thomas Durant and those staying here."

The beast relaxed. "Oh, Sir Denys. Forgive me for not recognizing you. I was just coming to check on them myself. Word on the street isn't good."

Denys dismounted. "Your name again?"

The beast bowed. "Enzo, sir."

Denys tilted his head back. "Ah, Enzo. Yes, of course. Now, please explain yourself."

"They were all supposed to leave several hours ago to head for the farm, but they were ambushed along the way."

Denys tensed. This was precisely why he was here. He had come to the same conclusion, that everyone should be moved to the farm, and with Marcus' concerns about keeping the Templars out of this situation, he had come to offer his men as an escort. "Any word on casualties?"

"From what we can gather, none before they left the city, except on Mr. Passe's side of things. Shortly after leaving the city, his men all returned in a hurry, and there were reports of a large column of Templars entering the city and returning to their fortress."

Denys smiled in relief. "So then, they are safe at the Fortress."

Enzo shook his head. "I'm afraid not, sir. According to Mrs. Thibault, women can't stay there after dark, and apparently Passe knows this as well. Word is spreading throughout the neighborhood that he and several other bosses are joining forces to attack the Templars when they move the women to the nunnery before dark. When I heard the calls, I immediately came here to see if Thomas or any of the others were hiding here."

Denys pointed to the door. "Go check. We need to be certain."

"Yes, sir." Enzo unlocked the door and disappeared inside.

Denys mounted his horse and turned to his marshal, Guillaume. "Send one of the men to intercept the column. I want them here at a gallop."

"Yes, sir." Marshal Guillaume pointed at one of his men. "You heard Sir Denys!"

"Yes, sir!" The man galloped off with the message for the rest of his personal guard, already on their way here, but at a much slower pace. The intention had been for him and a small guard to arrive, make the offer of an escort, then by the time Marcus and the others would be ready to leave, the rest of his men would arrive to head to the farm. But even with his foresight, with what might be happening, they could still arrive too late to help.

Enzo reemerged, shaking his head. "There's nobody here. All the supplies the Templars brought with them are gone, and Thomas appears to have packed for a lengthy stay at the farm."

If they weren't here, and they had left with enough time to pack properly, then that suggested a plan. And with the Templars having intervened, despite the fact that Marcus had indicated he didn't want the Order involved, it meant he must have changed his mind, recognizing the danger of remaining in Paris. "You said they're moving the women and children to the nunnery?"

"Mrs. Thibault and I believe so, sir."

"What children?"

"I don't know, sir. They just showed up this morning, apparently claiming their parents had been murdered and that their aunt was supposed to be coming to Thomas' residence."

Denys' eyes narrowed. "And who is this aunt?"

Enzo shrugged. "No idea. I only know the little I know because one of the squires came to collect Thomas at Mrs. Thibault's residence. My impression was that everything was happening quite quickly."

Denys scratched his chin. Based upon the timing, it would appear that Marcus and Simon had initiated a withdrawal from Paris immediately upon their return from visiting him. Marcus had evidently believed they might not make a clean getaway, so had arranged for help from the Order. He glanced up at the failing light then turned to Guillaume. "We must get to the Fortress and head off Sir Marcus. He might not be aware what is happening beyond the walls."

"Yes, sir."

Enzo looked up at him. "What can I do, sir?"

"Remain here. When my contingent arrives, tell them we headed to the Templar Fortress. Have them join me there at once."

"Yes, sir. You can count on me."

Denys bowed slightly. "I know I can." He urged his horse forward, his men leading the way as they charged through the strangely empty streets and toward the road that would lead them to the Fortress where he hoped he could begin to put an end to the chain of events that might lead to the destruction of the family of the woman he might just marry.

For after his conversation with François, he was convinced the man was having doubts about his chosen path, and together with Marcus, they might successfully appeal to him and put an end to this destructive road his potential father-in-law was racing down.

A road that could only lead to the ruination of his soul.

Leaving the Enclos du Temple, Templar Fortress
Paris, Kingdom of France

Thomas was terrified, his entire body trembling. And he wasn't alone. Isabelle sat huddled against him, shaking just as badly. Madeleine was across from them, her niece and nephew on either side, sobbing gently, unaware of what was going on, but fully aware that whatever it was had the adults scared.

All except for Simon, of course, who sat at the door of the wagon, guarding the only way in or out, mumbling curses the entire time at what he had called the "shit assignment." The man was a warrior who wanted to be outside in the thick of the battle to come, fighting by his master's side. Marcus had silenced his complaints, at least temporarily, with his explanation for the assignment.

"I need someone I can trust, that I know when all is lost, will fight to his last breath to save these people. I need you inside with them, my friend, because then I have no doubt that should I falter, they will live."

Simon had acquiesced at his master's explanation, muttering an apology for his characterization of his role in the mission.

The heavy war wagon picked up speed as they left the safety of the Fortress, every rut, every hole the wheels caught, jarring them all. Thomas could only imagine how uncomfortable it must be for Simon in his heavy equipment, though he had only ever heard the man complain about two things.

Manure and the cold.

The cold never really bothered Thomas, and now that he earned enough working for Thibault, his home always had a well-stoked fire. But the manure? He couldn't see how he'd ever get used to that. Isabelle's father had laughed about it, telling him that's why farmers had so many children so quickly. It was to pass off the nastiest chores.

Isabelle rested her head on his shoulder and he stared down at her golden hair. The very idea that he would be marrying a woman as beautiful as this, as sweet as this, would never have occurred to him, even just months ago. His mother was dead, his father murdered, leaving him destitute. He had no hopes, no prospects, no family. When Marcus and the others had found him, he was nearly starved, the charity of his neighbors only lasting so long. After his father's death, they had saved him, and through them, he had met Isabelle and Mrs. Thibault. He owed them his life. He owed them everything, yet he could never repay them.

Though there was one way. He could help work the farm. An extra set of hands during the busy growing season would lighten the load on these four men, all of whom were much older than him, and the thought had him vowing to embrace the work, rather than complain about it.

He placed a kiss on the top of Isabelle's head, his lips lingering as he breathed her in. He closed his eyes, imagining their future, a brood of children scurrying around a house they had built for themselves somewhere on either Marcus' property or her parents'. He wondered if he would ever be content enough to remain year-round at the farm, and give up his family home and all he had ever known. Could he keep his mind active enough to satisfy himself? Were there enough numbers involved in running a farm that the only talent he had could be made useful?

Figures filled his head of animals, how much they needed to be fed and when, where that feed would be sourced, how much it would cost to feed each animal per day, how much an animal could provide them through eggs, milk, and meat, how much the equivalent would cost at a market, and the more he thought about it, the bigger his smile became.

Perhaps life on a farm might not be so boring.

"Watch the rooftops!" yelled someone from outside, and his eyes shot open, reality shoving aside his daydream. Isabelle squeezed him tighter, her trembling mixing with his own. He noticed Simon was gripping the hilt of his sword tightly as he pressed his ear against the wood. Thomas did the same. He could hear the horses surrounding them changing position, men calling out to each other, issuing warnings, orders, some merely expressing concern. Something was about to happen, he was certain, but as Marcus had explained, there was no way anyone was getting in this wagon, and as long as it kept moving forward, they would reach the nunnery no matter what happened beyond these four walls.

There was a shout from up front, one of the coachmen. The horses whinnied in protest over something then the front of the wagon abruptly tipped forward. Everyone screamed including him, though Simon's scream was more accurately a curse as they came to a jarring halt that sent everyone hurtling toward the front of the wagon. He smacked his head against something unforgiving, and as he blacked out, a roar filled his ears that he prayed was imagined, for if it weren't, it sounded as if a hundred men or more were descending upon them.

Passe smiled with satisfaction as his perfectly laid plan unfolded. He had placed lookouts along the entire route, and the moment the wagon had left the gates, one of them had executed the coded call, passed on by the others. Once they were clear of the fortress walls, the shovels had hit the ground, a deep hole dug across the only road they could take, thin boards then placed over it and covered back up. It wasn't perfect, but at the speeds he hoped they would be traveling, it wouldn't be noticed until it was too late.

And he had been right. The two wheels of the front half of the carriage were now stuck in the hole, the entire fortress on wheels at a severe angle. There would be no getting it out without a team of horses, and it meant the Templars would have to make a stand here, stranded, against all the men he had amassed.

Including archers.

Two of his rivals on any other day stood on either side of him. Richart slapped him on the back. "I thought it a foolish idea, but it was brilliant!"

Olivier grinned in agreement. "I take back everything bad I've ever said about you."

Passe eyed him. "Everything?"

"Almost everything."

They all laughed as Passe initiated the next part of the plan by raising his hand in the air then dropping it toward the confused Templars. "Attack!"

Men swarmed from the alleyways, swords raised, creating a ring around the Templars, boxing them in with a wall of flesh, half a dozen men deep. Arrows rained down upon the trapped Templars from more than a dozen archers on the rooftops overhead as men on horseback buttressed the wall of flesh against retreat. Passe held out a hand and one of his men passed him a ceramic pot with a rag stuffed in the top. Passe stepped over to one of his men carrying a torch and lit the wick before heaving it at the carriage. It slammed into the side, the mixture of animal fat and alcohol it contained spreading out in every direction, coating the wood before erupting into a fireball. Screams from inside, women and children crying out in terror, confirmed to him that this was no decoy, this was no clever attempt at trickery by the Templars. Those he was after were indeed inside, and now they would be forced to come out.

And as Templars dropped before his eyes, the task became easier with each moment that passed. They would be victorious. The shared payday would be massive, but more importantly, his reputation in this city would be legend, and no one would ever dare challenge him again.

"Defensive positions!" shouted Marcus as he held his shield high, assessing the situation. They were boxed in for the moment. Screams erupted behind him and he turned back to see the war wagon on fire. He cursed. This wasn't a contingency he had planned for. This Passe was far more clever than he had assumed. The war wagon on fire, if it were moving, wasn't a great concern, for their trip to the nunnery wasn't long and the wood was thick. But the hole dug in the road, that he hadn't even noticed for his horse had galloped right over it, was ingenious, and had completely upended his plan.

The war wagon was now a liability.

He fell back, closer to the wagon. "Simon, are you all right in there?"

"Beginning to feel like I should be fitted for a spit!"

Marcus chuckled in relief. "Unlock the door and prepare to come outside."

"With pleasure, sir."

He could hear his sergeant grunting and cursing inside as he no doubt climbed toward the exit now at a difficult angle. "Thomas, is everyone else all right?" There was a hushed conversation before a reply.

"Yes, sir. We're all fine. Nobody appears seriously injured."

"Good." Marcus surveyed the scene. The knights and sergeants had formed a box surrounding the carriage, their shields raised high, protecting against the arrows that continued to rain upon them. A few of the targeted men were dragged within the box, and all appeared only injured. He peered out from behind his shield at the mass of humanity that surrounded them. They were men of varying ages, none in anything beyond leather armor, most carrying swords or daggers, none carrying them properly.

The aim of this was to overwhelm them and thin their numbers by way of the archers they had been missing in their first encounter. The plan could only work by stopping the carriage, which they had succeeded in doing, and by lighting it on fire, his people were now in an untenable position.

Those they were protecting would be exposed.

Marcus turned to one of the locally stationed

knights. "Which is closer, the Fortress or the nunnery?"

"The nunnery. We're barely a mile from there."

Marcus frowned as he spotted more locals surging into the area, a mishmash of drunks and vagabonds eager to participate in the mayhem, likely unaware as to what it was even about. Jealousies of the Templars weren't limited to nobility, and it appeared that a frenzy had been whipped up by Passe and his men, urging the entire area to take out their frustrations on the wealthy order. This would quickly get out of hand if they remained here.

Somebody screamed from above and to his left, and he smiled slightly as one of the enemy archers fell, gripping his stomach. He came to a decision and shouted over his shoulder. "Two rows of six archers up front! David, you command the first line, Jeremy the second!" A dozen squires rushed forward, forming two lines. "We need to create a path forward. Knights, use your shields to protect the archers. Archers, shoot under the horses. Advance after each volley. Sergeants, haul the bodies out of the way. Once the way is cleared, we get the passengers on horses and head for the nunnery. Understood?"

A chorus of "Yes, sirs" responded.

"David, at your discretion."

"Yes, sir!"

Marcus turned his attention to the war wagon, now almost fully engulfed, the coachmen struggling to free the horses. "Simon, make your exit now!"

The door swung open and Simon emerged. He reached inside and the small boy was lifted out. Simon passed him to one of the sergeants who handed him off to another. The little girl was next, then Isabelle,

Madeleine, and finally Thomas, blood trickling from his forehead. Simon jumped down and climbed on a horse brought forward by one of the squires as a group of sergeants surrounded them, their shields raised against the arrows that continued to fall.

Marcus cursed as he stood high in his saddle for a brief moment, checking on the progress ahead. David and Jeremy were clearing a path with their teams, but it wasn't the thinning crowd in front of them that had him concerned, it was those just ahead hauling debris across the road, further blocking their path.

His escape plan had yet again been hampered.

David's heart hammered at their desperate situation. He had been in battle before against countless thousands of Saracens hell-bent on gutting him and his fellow Christians, yet he couldn't remember a situation so desperate. They were hemmed in on two sides by buildings, the road now blocked in both directions, not just by walls of flesh, but debris as well. They weren't going anywhere quickly.

He breathed a sigh of relief when he checked over his shoulder to see Simon and the others were safely out of the war wagon, now fully ablaze, the heat from the flame warming his back. He scanned the rooftops, his bow at the ready, waiting for one of the enemy archers to show himself. Something moved to his left and he spun, loosing the arrow, his target crying out and collapsing out of sight. He and the other squires were far more skilled than their opponents, but they were outnumbered, and he feared the firepots used on the war wagon.

He had to act. He had to take the initiative.

"My line, fall back and watch the crowds for more of those firepots! Jeremy, your line continues forward!"

He fell back with his archers as Jeremy's advanced, continuing to thin the crowd ahead of them. They were making rapid progress and should soon break through, but if there were more of this new weapon just introduced into the battle, they could be done for. He made for the wall of Templars to his right, still mounted on their armored horses, their shields held high. He dropped to the ground, his bow parallel to the muddy ground and peered at the crowd, checking faces for those who were too calm as they prepared for something horrible, but more importantly, checking hands.

He had seen the ceramic pot in the air before it smashed into the side of the war wagon. It would take two hands to light one. He ignored anyone holding a sword or a dagger or any other implement meant for cutting or smashing. He continued his rapid scan then stopped, pulling his arrow back slightly to the right. Three men were standing in an alley who appeared out of place. He squinted in the failing light. He couldn't be certain, but the one in the middle, he could swear, had been the one Thomas had identified as Passe, and he, along with the others, were holding ceramic pots, a man behind them with a torch lighting the wicks.

"Archers, shoot on the alleyway to the right!" He loosed his arrow and quickly grabbed another of his dwindling supply from his quiver as the archers around him struggled to find the target.

If they didn't act fast, this could be the end for them all.

Passe was impressed. The Templars had swiftly regrouped, forming a defensive line that effectively neutralized his archers, but the plan had worked. The wagon had been stopped, and now the rear door was open and everyone he was after was now outside. The moment he saw what the Templars were attempting, he had ordered the roads blocked in front and behind, delaying any possible escape.

These Templars were going nowhere.

And the women and children were his.

Now that they were exposed, it was time for the final part of his plan. He raised his hand, as did Richart and Olivier, each carrying another ceramic pot filled with animal fat and alcohol. Bertaut walked past with a torch, lighting each of theirs along with half a dozen more held by men behind them. "On three!" He raised his weapon over his head. "One! Two!"

Olivier cried out and Passe checked to see what was the matter as his rival collapsed to his knees. An arrow had pierced his arm, and as the wounded man reached for it, he dropped the pot.

"No!" Passe cried as he whipped his toward the Templars then spun on his heel. Olivier's pot shattered at his feet, the flammable liquid surging from its confines, spreading across the ground, the wick igniting the deadly concoction. Olivier screamed in agony as he was engulfed in flames. Richart's leg caught fire, and he too roared from the excruciating pain.

Passe dove to the ground as the heat from the flame washed over him. He rolled over onto his back and pushed up on his elbows. His eyes bulged at his foot aflame. Bertaut rushed over and dropped to his knees, scooping mud onto the fire, quickly extinguishing it, then hauled his master to his feet. Passe smacked him on the arm. "Thanks, I owe you one."

Bertaut grinned. "I could use a new knife."

Passe laughed at the reference to the bejeweled dagger still hanging on the wall in his office as they took cover in a doorway, the Templar archers focusing their arrows on their position. Olivier was fully engulfed now, his cries thankfully silenced, and one of Richart's men had shoved the panicking man to the ground, copying Bertaut's method of putting out the fire. He appeared relatively unscathed, though might disagree once he discovered the extent of his burns.

The others had all pulled their wicks in the panic, uncertain as to what to do. Passe pointed at them. "Relight those and get them on the Templars! Look at what just two have done!"

Everyone turned to see the effects of his own device that he had hurled at the last moment, and the first tossed at the war wagon, and it had smiles spreading throughout the group as they realized this was the key to victory.

Marcus cursed at a warning cry from one of the knights to his right. He turned and spotted another of the firepots sailing toward them, its flaming wick spinning in the failing light. "Raise shields!" he shouted, and any who didn't already have theirs raised lifted them higher. The firepot shattered against one of the shields, the flames exploding outward in a brilliant flash. Those affected tossed their shields back toward the crowd before the fire could spread to them or their horse.

"Form up!" ordered Marcus, and the gaps were quickly filled with sergeants as mud was kicked onto the flaming liquid, several of those on the front line rolling in the ground to put out the flames. As they were helped by their comrades, David's archers were shooting in the direction of where the device had come from, and he spotted flames in the alleyway, suggesting their enemy had become victim to their own weapons.

But it also meant there were more.

They had to get out of here, and they had to get out of here now. He turned to Jeremy. "Clear us that path! We're out of time!"

"Yes, sir! Advance!" shouted Jeremy, the wall of knights in front of them moving forward, the horses trampling the bodies of the archers' victims. A group of sergeants rushed forward, dragging the corpses and the wounded out of the way. Marcus glanced to his right to make certain that the women and children and Thomas were all right. They were on the ground now, huddled together, surrounded by a wall of horses, sergeants, and shields, including Simon. The arrows from overhead continued, though there were far fewer now as David's archers took them out as they revealed themselves to loose their shots.

This was not going according to plan. The wagon was never supposed to have been stopped. This was warfare unlike any he had fought. His engagements were almost always in the desert, the wide-open expanses never permitting such a tactic. This city warfare was different, and the next time it happened, he'd account for that. But there was no time to think about what had gone wrong. That would be for tomorrow, assuming they should survive the day.

And at this very moment, he wasn't so sure if they would.

The screams and cries of battle were just ahead. Horses protested, men shouted, swords clashed, the horrors of war revealed through just his ears. Denys brought his men to a halt and dismounted, rather than charging into a battle where they could be hopelessly outnumbered. He peered around the corner and cursed. He could see the Templar colors ahead, a war wagon aflame, their path blocked by a mass of humanity wielding swords, daggers, and other weapons of convenience. There was no way the five of them could engage in any useful manner. He needed his full guard. Only then could they make a difference.

People were coming in from all directions, some merely curious onlookers, others misfits eager to join in on a brawl. This was quickly getting out of hand, but his men were at least five minutes away, if not more. There were too many for his escort to engage, but once the bulk of his force arrived, it would be formidable, certainly against untrained opponents. As more continued to pour into the area, he could think of only one thing that might help. He pointed at the road. "Let's block this so no one else can get through to join the fight."

"Yes, sir," said Guillaume, directing his small force, and within moments, a wall of beasts and men with swords drawn blocked access to the fight, at least from this one direction, his marshal barking at anyone who approached, ordering them to return from whence they came.

Denys stared back at the Templars, furiously battling against overwhelming odds, then gasped in horror as several objects sailed through the air and erupted in flame, adding to the already burning catastrophe unfolding before his eyes. He cursed then prayed to the Lord to have his men arrive soon.

Enclos du Temple, Templar Fortress
Paris, Kingdom of France

Sir Matthew stood in one of the turrets of the massive wall surrounding the Templar Fortress, peering into the failing light. Marcus should have arrived at the nunnery by now as it was a short distance on nearly empty streets, but no messenger had arrived. Something was wrong. Somebody had reported seeing a flash in the distance that had drawn him to his current position. He could see a dull glow, but it could be anything.

Several flashes in a row removed any doubt in his mind as to what was going on. His men were under attack by incendiary devices that he hadn't seen used since his days battling the Saracens in the Holy Lands. He leaned over the wall into the central courtyard. "Prepare twenty knights for battle! Our people are under attack!"

"Yes, sir," responded someone from below who rushed off to execute his order. Matthew turned back to stare in the distance, and now that he knew where he was looking, he could distinctly see the smoke billowing into what would soon be a pitch-black sky. If a fire that large were raging, it had to mean the war wagon had come under attack, but how, he couldn't fathom. There should have been no way for it to have been stopped. Something must have gone horribly wrong.

He rushed down the stairs and into the courtyard, barking orders for a full alert, the order repeated throughout the fortress as every able man scrambled to prepare for battle. Matthew entered the main complex, pointing at one of his squires. "Prepare my armor. I'm heading into battle."

"At once, sir." His squire rushed off to make preparations as Matthew marched after him, clearing his mind of the administrative trivialities that normally preoccupied him, centering himself for the task ahead. Marcus hadn't wanted the Order to become involved, but now they were, and with the size of their intervention and who was involved, it could mean yet another confrontation with the King.

Scene of the Battle
Paris, Kingdom of France

Enzo heard the screams and cries of battle just down the road. He desperately wanted to go and help, but he had his orders. He already had a hatchet in one hand, a barbed club in the other, waiting for the moment Sir Denys' men arrived. It was taking too long, and he debated leaving, as those he was waiting for to arrive would undoubtedly hear the fight just ahead and investigate.

He thought he heard something over the din and cocked an ear, smiling at the sound of scores of hooves approaching. He stepped out into the road as at least a dozen men on horseback, fully armored, appeared. He waved his hands over his head as the column came to a halt.

"Where did they go?" asked the man in the lead, dispensing with any pleasantries as he must have sensed Enzo's urgency.

Enzo pointed in the direction of the fight. "They went that way, toward the Templar Fortress, but I'm guessing they've been caught up in the fight. You should be able to hear it."

The man listened for a moment then cursed, turning in his saddle. "Leave the cart here!" he ordered before signaling the advance. The horses galloped past and Enzo sprinted after them, his lumbering form not designed for speed. He could see smoke ahead, and as he rounded a bend, he roared in rage as he spotted flaming pots sailing through the air and into a crossroad where he had no doubt the Templars were trapped.

There was no defending against fire.

He leaned into his sprint, noticing every window of the houses around him were filled with curious onlookers. He reached the crowd and pushed through, peering around the corner, and his jaw dropped. Sir Denys' men were engaged in the narrow confines of the street, battling at least a dozen men on horseback that he recognized as a combination of several gangs from the area. Farther down the road, he could see the Templar colors and what appeared to be an armored wagon engulfed in flames.

He pushed through the onlookers whose morbid curiosity outweighed the danger they might be putting themselves in, and as he neared the melee between Sir Denys' guard and Passe's temporary alliance, another flaming ball sailed through the air, exploding near the Templars' position.

And it reminded him of when Thomas' house had been torched.

His eyes widened as he remembered that day, and what had happened next. He ducked down an alleyway, cutting back to a parallel street, then made his way to the row of houses opposite where the Templars were hemmed in. He grabbed a man standing nearby by the shirt that he recognized as a local, not a gang member. "We need a bucket brigade. Now!"

The man stared at him blankly. "What?"

"We need a bucket brigade." Enzo pointed to the building. "Through this house to the second floor, so we can throw the water on the Templars."

"I don't want to get involved."

Enzo raised a fist. "Bucket brigade. Now!"

The man's eyes bulged as he gulped then sprinted off toward the nearby well. Enzo stepped out from the building, peering up at the windows all around him, many with their shutters closed for the night, others filled with curious onlookers.

"The Templars need our help! We need a bucket brigade!"

"To hell with the Templars!" shouted someone.

Enzo spun toward the voice. "These Templars are protecting your friends, your neighbors. They're protecting women and children. You all should be ashamed of yourselves for allowing it to come to this. They're fighting to stop the King and his lords from stealing our children, from kidnapping our babies. You know the Templars have never done us any harm. It's the King who spits on his subjects. Help me now. Help me help them. We need a bucket brigade, or they and the women and children they are fighting to protect, will all die, and their blood will be on your hands for just sitting there and staring out your windows."

His heart sank as his words fell on deaf ears, but after a few moments, a door finally opened to his left and a man stepped out with his two sons. The father nodded at Enzo, who returned the gesture, then pointed at the family. "Are they the only ones? Are they the only good Christians among you? Are they all that stands for justice in this neighborhood?"

Another door opened, then another, men, women, and children emerging as the windows emptied. Enzo pointed to the well where the first man was pumping. "We need a fire brigade from the well to the second floor. We'll be throwing the water through the windows onto the fight below."

The neighborhood sprang into action and Enzo stepped back for a moment, his chest swelling in pride as so many put their lives at risk to do the right thing because of words he had spoken. It was a feeling he had never experienced before, for he rarely had an opportunity to do anything truly good. The first bucket was rushed up to him. He climbed the porch of the building between them and the Templars. The door opened, an elderly woman stepping aside, and he paused.

She stared up at him. "Well, what are you waiting for? Are you a man of only words?"

Enzo grinned and stepped into the house. Rushing up the stairs directly ahead of him, he threw open the shutters on the window and gasped in horror at the sight below.

Marcus yanked one of the knights off his horse, throwing him to the ground, squires scrambling to put out the fire that now engulfed him, the animal fat used in the firepot coating his armor, providing fuel for the flame. They wouldn't last much longer, and they still couldn't clear the path ahead as those they removed from the blockade were replaced just as quickly.

"Sir, look ahead!" yelled Jeremy.

Marcus adjusted his shield, his shoulder now in agony as he peered ahead, beyond the crowd thwarting their progress, beyond the debris strewn across the road. He spotted five men on horseback blocking their path to escape yet again, then he smiled as he recognized the colors.

It was Sir Denys.

He had to think they were holding their position

because they didn't have enough men to engage, but by doing so, they were cutting off some of the reinforcements being sent in to hold the line while this war of attrition slowly took its toll. Another volley was tossed, exploding once again on the shields, and as each one did, the man holding it was forced to toss it away, reducing their protection from not only these firepots, but from the archers above.

"Sir Marcus, to your left!"

Marcus swung his shield and the ceramic shattered on the other side, a whoosh of heat and flame shooting out from all sides as he ducked behind it. He tossed his shield aside then fell back as the gap was filled. Flames surrounded them now, and as the number of wounded increased, their defensive line continued to thin.

Suddenly he was hit by a large amount of liquid. He closed his eyes, drawing in a deep breath in anticipation of the flame, and when none came, he licked his lips and discovered it was water. The man beside him was drenched as well, and Marcus looked up and silently cried out his thanks to God at the beastly Enzo in a window above, tossing out a bucketful of water before disappearing and reappearing with a fresh one. Two more windows were thrown open, more people appearing, each with bucket in hand, tossing the precious liquid onto the burning fires below. His heart filled with joy at the sight of these commoners risking their lives to help them.

And they had to take advantage, as there was no telling how long these brave people would be allowed to continue. He turned and spotted his squire lying on the ground, searching for a target. "David, redirect your archers to the front!"

"Yes, sir!"

The archers repositioned, joining Jeremy's, and Marcus could sense the boost in morale sweeping over his beleaguered men.

They might just yet survive this.

Enzo dumped yet another bucket down on the Templars below, smiling at Sir Marcus giving him a salute before returning to the fight. If someone had told him a year ago that one day he would be helping Templars in battle, he would have thought them a fool, and might have bloodied their nose for suggesting he'd help knights battle his own kind. Yet here he was, and it felt good.

"There's a problem outside!" somebody shouted from down the stairs.

Enzo spun toward the man beside him. "You take over, just keep getting the water on them."

"Yes, sir." The man carried the bucket already in his hands to the window as Enzo rushed down the stairs, squeezing past the others, and emerging into the night. A scream to his left had him spinning and he spotted several of Passe's group threatening the men and women of the neighborhood, the bucket line quickly collapsing. He yanked his hatchet and club off his belt and roared as he rushed toward the men. He was entering a sword fight woefully ill-equipped, but he didn't care. He had to protect these people, for they were in danger because he had urged them to fight back.

He surged into the melee, swinging his hatchet, splitting open the head of his nearest opponent, while the club, its deadliness enhanced with metal spikes driven through it, clawed off half a man's face. He raised his foot, kicking off the body attached to his hatchet, sending it flying against the side of a nearby house as the blade already swung, cleaving off his next victim's arm. The last of the men scurried away, their swords left behind as Enzo, his chest heaving, slowly spun, searching for anyone else who would threaten these innocent people. Finding none, he stood in the middle of the street.

"It's safe now! Let's get back to work! And anyone who dares interfere will get the same treatment that filth did!"

Cheers erupted from the men and women surrounding him, some of the children rushing over to pat him, smiling up at him in awe, none recoiling from his horribly mangled face. He swelled from the love shown, as, for the first time in his life, he felt human.

And it was wonderful.

Passe Residence
Paris, Kingdom of France

François arrived at Passe's residence and found the front door locked. He hammered on the heavy wood, but no one answered. He was late, his detour to the church having delayed him more than he had anticipated, though it was worth it. He might have saved his soul, though only if he could stop what he had set in motion. He hammered again on the door, refusing to believe that a man such as this kept the hours of a baker.

"Who is it?" asked a woman on the other side.

He was about to say his name when he stopped. "I have business with Mr. Passe."

"He's not here right now. Come back tomorrow."

"But I have an appointment to see him today."

"Is that you, your Lordship?"

François gulped. She had used his title, but did that really mean anything? In her ignorance, she might not know what to properly call him. But who was she? The only woman he had encountered in this nasty business was the woman who had handed him the baby. "Do I know you?"

The door opened a sliver and a provocatively dressed woman appeared. "I thought I recognized your voice." She smiled, and he was relieved it was indeed the same woman from the other night. "Here for a little sugar?" She grabbed her breasts and heaved them up before letting go and giving them a bounce.

He gulped, never before having seen such a display. "Umm, no, I'm here to pay Mr. Passe, and to call off the job I hired him to do."

Her eyes shot wide. "Call off?" She laughed. "I'm afraid it's too late for that, milord."

"What do you mean?"

"I mean he's already out there putting an end to your problem."

His chest tightened. "I don't understand."

"The boss found your missing maid and found the children. They're fighting the Templars right now. He even got Richart and Olivier and all of his men in on it. It's the biggest battle this neighborhood's ever seen, from what I've been told."

A young boy appeared at her side. "It is, sir. I just came back from there. It's unbelievable! It's like nothing I've ever seen."

François paled. "Where is this happening?"

The woman pushed the boy out the door. "Show him."

"Yes, ma'am."

The woman eyed François, her eyes roaming his body as if searching for something. "There was mention of a payment?"

François gave her a look. "I'll pay Passe and no one else."

She frowned. "Nobody ever trusts me." She slammed the door and the young man stood by, hopping up and down on his toes with impatience, clearly eager to get back to witness the battle. François mounted his horse and held out an arm, swinging the boy onto the back.

"Which way?"

The boy pointed ahead and François urged his horse forward, the boy directing them along the way.

"How much is a thousand deniers?"

François' eyes narrowed. "What do you mean?"

"How much is a thousand deniers? It's the reward I'm going to get for having found the woman and the children."

François' tensed at the second mention of children. "What children are you talking about?"

"The niece and nephew of the maid."

His heart ached and his chest burned. This was all his fault. He had given the order. Passe had explicitly asked him what should happen if the secret were revealed to others, and the vile man must believe the children had been told. He tilted his head back and cried out. "Why, Lord, why?"

"What's wrong, milord?"

François' chin collapsed to his chest as the tears flowed freely. He coughed, then coughed again. He reached into an inner pocket and withdrew a handkerchief as the cough turned into a fit. The horse continued forward as he dropped the reins while he struggled to breathe, fluid filling his lungs, blood spattering the cloth held to his mouth. His horse, no longer under his control, picked up speed while its master gave confusing signals from the saddle as his barking cough, more severe than any he had ever experienced, overwhelmed him.

"Milord, are you all right?"

"No," he managed to gasp.

The boy reached around him and grabbed the reins,

pulling back, bringing the horse to a halt. He jumped down to the ground, staring up at him. "What should I do?"

"Get help."

The boy nodded then sprinted off, and as the coughing fit continued, François collapsed in his saddle, the world going dark around him.

Scene of the Battle
Paris, Kingdom of France

"Sir, they're here!"

Denys spun in his saddle at the call from Guillaume and sighed in relief at the sight of his personal guard galloping toward them from around the bend. As the column came to a halt, he pointed with his sword toward the battle. "We have one job, and that's to clear a path between here and the Templars so they can make their escape. Consider anyone not wearing a Templar uniform the enemy. Understood?"

A chorus of "Yes, sirs" replied.

He raised his sword in the air and yelled, "In our Lord's name, we fight!" He lowered the blade and charged forward, his men spreading out behind him, creating a wall of man and beast that filled the roadway from side to side. Those piling the debris turned toward the approaching danger, eyes bulging at the mounted cavalry rushing their position. Denys came to a halt, indicating for his men to surround the barricade. He thrust his sword toward one of the men cowering before them. "You and the others will remove this immediately. When I return, I'll gut every last one of you if this road isn't open!"

The man shook out a terrified nod then went to work, the others quickly joining in. Denys pointed at two of his men. "Remain here and make sure they do their job. Kill anyone who tries to leave."

"Yes, sir!"

Denys charged forward with the rest of his men, and

within moments, were engaged directly in the desperate battle being waged.

And he hadn't felt so alive in years.

Marcus glanced up, noticing the buckets of water being tossed on them had stopped. Someone in one of the windows gestured, indicating they didn't know what was wrong. But the several dozen buckets that had doused the flames had made all the difference. The ground they fought upon was now slick with mud, reducing the risk.

Another firepot sailed in and he raised his shield taken from one of the fallen sergeants. The flame flashed over its surface and he shoved it into the muck, extinguishing it with a hiss. Shouts from ahead had him turning to see over a dozen of Sir Denys' men engaging the crowd blocking their path. Those at the back were quickly dispatched, revealing what was truly happening. The enemy facing them were being forced into the situation. A line of Passe's men in the rear were shoving them forward, replacements funneled in from the alleyways at knifepoint. With Denys' men blocking the route for several minutes, the numbers had dwindled, and now that Passe's men were fully engaged, those that hadn't escaped earlier were now peeling off from the group in ones and twos, sprinting past Passe's men and Denys' guard, who let them go unscathed.

"Prepare to advance!" he shouted as he mounted his horse. All around him, knights and sergeants mounted their steeds as the archers continued to engage on foot. A bucket of water splashed nearby and he glanced up at the windows above to see another tossed out. Enzo's efforts were once again underway. He glanced over his shoulder at his sergeant. "Simon, report!"

"All present and accounted for, sir!"

"Let's keep it that way." Marcus raised his sword as he made eye contact with Denys, the nobleman's blade slicing through the air, blood spraying as his target was felled. A gap in the mass of beast and man revealed the road ahead, mostly cleared of the debris blocking it, two of Denys' men forcing Passe's people to clear the debris under threat of evisceration. Marcus urged his horse forward, the massive weight of the beast in its armor shoving through the thin crowd now blocking them. He swung his blade, slicing open the chest of one who seemed determined to continue the engagement, but the regrouped Templars pressed forward, crushing those who stood their ground, and within moments they were finally through.

"It would appear we arrived just in time," said Denys, turning his horse to ride alongside.

"Indeed, your timing is most fortunate."

"What do you want us to do?"

"We'll pass through. You cover our backs to the nunnery at a slower pace. Once our charges are inside, we'll come back to assist should there be any trouble. We'll regroup then return to clean up this mess."

"Very well." Denys turned to his marshal. "Did you hear that?"

"Yes, sir, we'll cover the rear."

Marcus continued forward, past the now mostly removed blockade. The crowds ahead were gone, the streets empty as the sounds of mayhem continued behind him. He pulled his horse over to the side, waving for everyone else to continue. Simon and a group of sergeants passed with Thomas, Isabelle, and the others in their midst. He joined them, covering them from behind. David and Jeremy galloped up beside him, their bows still at the ready, watching the rooftops.

It didn't take long for the walls of the nunnery to come into sight. The gates opened and the Templars in the lead broke off to the left and right, turning their horses. Simon blasted through, followed by the others, and the moment they cleared, Marcus breathed a sigh of relief and turned his horse around. He yanked his surcoat off and tossed it to David, then did the same with his tunic. He threw his shield with its Templar crest to the ground. David, realizing what was happening, rushed over and cut the caparison from the horse, as there was no time to remove the saddle and do it properly. As Marcus stood high in his saddle, free of all the obvious symbols of their venerated order, others around him did the same, for what they were about to do now was not in the name of the Order, but in the name of justice.

As knights, sergeants, and squires rode by, at least half of them injured, several worse, more turned to join him. Simon rode up, stripping out of his trappings as he approached.

"You didn't think you were going to leave without me, did you?"

Marcus chuckled. "I figured you'd be able to find us."

"What's the plan?"

Marcus turned to the men that remained, a mix of knights, sergeants, and squires. "Passe is still out there. I want him and whoever else was responsible for what just happened."

David spoke up. "Sir, when I saw Passe, he was with two men that were dressed in fine clothes as well. I believe one of them was badly burned, but I'm guessing they were the three behind this."

Marcus agreed. "This was definitely the work of more than just Passe. According to the intelligence briefing I received, he didn't have enough men."

Denys' men arrived, the man slumping in his saddle, exhausted. He hailed Marcus with a limply raised hand. "I fear, my friend, I'm in no condition for sustained battle."

Marcus smiled, slapping the man on his armor. "My friend, if it weren't for you, none of us might be here now. Go home. Your job is done."

Denys shook his head. "Our job is done when yours is."

Marcus shook his head. "No. What just happened can be excused by you coming to the assistance of men in need. Your king cannot fault you for that. But what comes next may involve members of his court, and trust me when I say, there's a very good chance the King will not be happy with what's about to happen."

Denys sighed. "Very well. I have some wounded that must be tended to. I will take my leave of you. Good luck, Sir Marcus."

"And to you, Sir Denys."

Denys turned his horse and his men charged back toward the battle and the road that would lead them across the river to where men like him called home.

Marcus turned to the others. "We seek a man named Passe. He is a crime boss in this area who traffics in children."

Muttered curses rippled through the men who had

never been told of the reason for the mission they had just been through.

"We seek him and the others like him to not only send them on to the next life where God can mete out the justice He sees fit, but also to put the fear of God into those who would dare think to commit such a crime in the future. We do this not in the name of our order, but as knights who swore to protect the innocent, and as men who cannot just stand by while the innocent are victimized." He thrust his blood-soaked sword into the air, rising in his saddle. "Tonight, in the name of our Lord, we fight for those who cannot fight for themselves, and deliver God's justice upon this earth!"

A roar erupted from the men, and it reminded him of the field of battle in the Holy Lands, where thousands upon thousands would have been shouting, the entire ground rumbling in fear of the power represented. He directed his sword back toward the battle that had been, and dropped into his saddle, urging his horse forward. She reared on her hind legs, then surged ahead, followed by the others determined to seek revenge for what had just happened, and to put the fear of God into any who would even think about victimizing children.

Approaching the Scene of the Battle
Paris, Kingdom of France

Gerart rushed toward the battle raging not far from here. People were streaming into the area, people he recognized as the worst of the worst. Others were fleeing. Some women, many carrying children.

And he froze.

The screams and cries and clashing of swords, along with the smell of smoke, of burning wood, of burning meat, had him questioning what he was doing. This was because of him. He had found the children. If he and his friends hadn't spotted them, they might have gotten away safely. But in his greed, in his desire to save himself from the life he was now living, he had condemned others to death, and by the sounds of it, perhaps scores.

This was all his fault.

He bent over and emptied his stomach. He couldn't be part of this. It wasn't right. It wasn't him. It wasn't the way he had been raised. He turned back in the direction of the nobleman he had just left. He sounded as if he were dying and the man needed help. But he couldn't go to Passe. He wanted nothing to do with the man anymore, yet it was his Christian duty to help. But what could he do?

He turned, facing down the street to his left. He didn't know what to do, though he knew who might. He sprinted toward the only home he had ever known, toward the only place he had ever felt safe, and to the only man who always had the answers.

His father.

Passe stopped to catch his breath, ducking into an alleyway as a massive column of Templar soldiers rushed past the scene of the battle, reinforcements from the Fortress finally arriving. He had been winning the fight. It was only a matter of time before they would have been victorious, yet they had been betrayed. Not by the personal guard of some nobleman, but by the people of the neighborhood he ruled. It was those who had helped douse the flames that had saved the Templars and those they were protecting. If it weren't for the vermin that were supposed to cower in fear at his feet, his firepots would have continued to burn and eventually found their mark.

As the Templars cleared past, he walked back toward the scene of the battle. Not a Templar was in sight, not even their dead. Nor were any of the noblemen's guard. All that remained were the men that belonged to him, Richart, and Olivier, along with scores of wounded or dead locals forced into the battle. He glanced up to see buckets of water still pouring down on the scene, most directed at the war wagon that still stubbornly burned.

He growled in frustration and turned to the smattering of men he had left. "Let's go see who's behind this." He stormed around the side of the building and nearly ran into Bertaut.

"Sir, we might have a problem!"

Passe frowned, tossing his hand back toward their failure. "You mean something worse than this?"

Bertaut shrugged. "I don't know how to answer that."

Passe growled in frustration. "Out with it. What's this problem?"

"Olivier's men are blaming us for his death."

Passe tensed. Olivier was a worthy rival, though didn't have as many men as he did. Both their numbers were weakened today, and the question was, who was weakened more? "What about Richart?"

"He just left with his men. He's blaming you too. I think the two are going to unite against us. He just welcomed any of Olivier's men into his group if they want to join."

"How many do you think we're facing?"

"Twenty, maybe thirty."

Passe frowned as they rounded the corner, revealing the bucket brigade that had turned the tide of the battle, water its only weapon. He indicated for the others to spread out. "Kill as many as you can. Let's send a message that no one interferes in our business."

Swords that weren't already drawn slid from their scabbards, Passe leaving his weapon sheathed, instead clenching his fists, thirsty for blood. He strode forward rapidly, the others flanking him on both sides. A woman screamed as she spotted them, and the crowd turned. His men charged but their prey fled in every direction, most ducking down alleyways, quickly lost in the dark. The night was upon them, the only light from torches brought out for the occasion, the glow cast upward of the war wagon on the opposite side of the building, and the faint moonlight. His men scattered after them as he clenched his fists harder, enraged at yet another failure. Slowly he turned, seeking someone to fight, and his eyes bulged, a flood of fear rushing through his body as he spotted a massive beast coming toward him.

He squinted and cursed as he recognized Enzo barreling toward him, his own monster-sized fists hanging by his sides. Passe resisted the urge to take a step back, and instead squared himself against the man, stabbing a finger at him. "I have no quarrel with you, Enzo. Walk away."

Enzo continued marching forward and Passe's resistance proved futile, his body involuntarily retreating two steps.

He again stabbed the air between them. "Mrs. Thibault and I have no quarrel. Don't create a problem where there is none."

Enzo raised his fists. "Mrs. Thibault doesn't know I'm here and has nothing to do with this. This is between you and me. This is for trying to kill my friends."

"Enzo!" snapped a voice from the shadows that Passe recognized as Thibault's. The lumbering beast stopped and Passe quickly assessed his escape routes. He was about to dart down an alley when he smiled, two of his men returning. He directed them to get behind Enzo, and they warily obeyed his orders. Another two appeared and another. The tide had quickly turned. It was no longer man against beast, it was man and his ten friends against the beast. Even the mighty Enzo had no hope of surviving those odds.

Thibault strode out onto the street, putting herself between Passe and her enforcer. "What's going on here?"

"What's going on is that your man interfered in my business."

"Oh? Did you, Enzo, interfere with Mr. Passe's

business?"

"I was merely helping put out a fire before it got out of control, ma'am."

Thibault turned back toward Passe. "Is your business setting fire to the neighborhood?"

Passe raised a finger in protest, but she cut him off.

"Because we all live in this neighborhood, and from what I've heard tell of, something most irresponsible was done here today while conducting your business. I don't care if you kill Templars. I don't care if you kill those who interfere with your business. But I do care when what you do threatens the residents in this neighborhood that both of us rely upon for that very business."

Richart emerged from an alleyway with several dozen men behind him. He approached the two of them, his hand on the hilt of his dagger. He bowed slightly at Thibault. "It's good to see you, Mrs. Thibault. I hope the evening finds you well."

Thibault acknowledged him. "I'm surprised to see you here. Please tell me you're not in league with this creature."

Richart stared at Passe, a frown creasing his face. "I was foolish enough to believe his lies, as was Olivier."

Thibault looked about. "Where is that scoundrel?"

"He's dead."

An eyebrow cocked on Thibault's forehead. "Dead? How?"

"He caught fire when one of those wretched firepots was accidentally dropped."

Thibault shook her head, eying Passe. "You see what I mean? Most irresponsible."

Passe raised a fist at her and Richart's dagger was drawn several inches as Enzo growled. Passe relaxed his stance slightly. "This is none of your concern, madam. I suggest you and your man withdraw."

Richart agreed. "This is now between him and me. I suggest you withdraw and remain neutral in this matter."

Thibault nodded. "I agree, gentlemen. This is none of my concern." She turned and beckoned Enzo to follow. "Let's let these two men settle their differences." They disappeared into the shadows, a dozen others leaving with them, Thibault evidently not out undefended.

Passe turned to face Richart, his fists once again clenched. "You and me, Richart."

Richart smiled. "Oh, I think you're mistaken, my friend. I'm not fool enough to go up against those iron fists of yours." He raised a hand over his shoulder, a lone finger beckoning. "It's my men against your men. Whoever's left standing controls the neighborhood."

Passe resisted the urge to just run. He glanced over each shoulder, reconfirming what he already knew. He had perhaps a dozen men, and he was facing triple that. They didn't stand a chance. "Let's get the hell back home," he hissed.

"You don't have to tell me twice," said Bertaut as they slowly retreated, swords held out warily as the united forces of Richart and Olivier advanced on them.

A horse neighed behind him.

"Going somewhere?"

He spun to find four men on horseback blocking their path. They had no markings, but their equipment was exceptional, and all were covered in mud and blood. These were Templars. There could be no doubt. His heart was hammering now, and only bravado would get him through this. "Withdraw now, Templar, or I'll inform the King that you interfered in the business of his subjects."

The man who had spoken sneered at him. "A dead man's tongue cannot wag its lies."

Marcus urged his horse forward several steps, the others doing the same, forcing Passe backward. He had come to find Enzo in case he was in trouble after helping them, but instead had encountered Thibault and her men, word having already reached her not only of the battle, but the result, a result he couldn't be more pleased with. The fact that one of the bosses he had wanted brought to justice was already dead, and the remaining two were about to fight things out to the death, suited him just fine.

"What should we do?" Simon had asked, itching to bloody his sword.

"We let them kill each other."

It was the perfect solution to the problem. He only had to make certain the fight took place. He had let Thibault retrieve Enzo while his men positioned themselves around the area, blocking all the exits, caging in the two rival groups so there'd be no escape.

And now they watched.

Somebody shouted from the other side of the street, finally noticing the men on horseback with no markings hemming them in.

"What the hell is going on here?" shouted the man identified to him as Richart. "What treachery is this?" He drew his dagger, glaring at Passe. "You ally yourself with our enemy? Was this all a trick from the beginning?"

Richart charged forward, swinging his blade at Passe, who ducked and delivered an uppercut that had his opponent sailing backward several feet then sliding in the mud, coming to a halt out cold. Richart's men charged, swords and daggers swinging, and Passe's men responded.

And within moments, the battle Marcus had been hoping for now raged.

"Is this what you wanted?" asked a voice from behind.

He turned and acknowledged Thibault and Enzo. "It serves my purpose, but let it be known to all, that should I find out anyone has kidnapped a child, I or one of my fellow Templars will take action and dispatch them to burn in Hell."

Thibault bowed slightly. "I'll make sure that word gets around. Now, I think I'll take my leave of you, Templar. Until we meet again."

Marcus bowed in his saddle. "Until we meet again, ma'am."

She turned and walked away, but Enzo lingered. "Please let Thomas and Isabelle know that I am pleased they are well, and that I will see them at the house when they feel it is safe to do so."

Marcus smiled at the man's concern. "You have my word, my friend." He pointed toward the scene of the previous battle. "And you have my thanks."

Enzo shrugged. "I was just putting out a fire."

Marcus laughed and Enzo flashed a grin before rushing off to catch up to Thibault and the others. Marcus returned his attention to the battle, taking great satisfaction in the fact half of those involved had already been taken out.

Simon growled beside him. "Is my sword to remain dry tonight?"

Marcus shrugged. "God works in mysterious ways. If it's His desire that these men deliver justice upon themselves, then who are we to question His will?"

Simon jabbed a finger at Passe. "Promise me one thing."

"What's that?"

"If he's the last man standing, he's mine."

"By sword or by fist? He seems quite handy without a blade in his hand."

Simon spat. "Fist it is."

Denys rode past the aftermath of the battle and turned up the road that would lead past Thomas Durant's house where they could retrieve their wagon and load their wounded. He was exhausted, yet more alive than he had felt in months. Though he'd pay for it tomorrow. He had no doubt his entire body would be aching, but he and his men had done good. They had turned the tide in the desperate battle, helping save innocent women and children and valiant Templars. It was a good day, and would hopefully put an end to François' folly. Surely after what had happened, there was no way the man would continue.

They rounded a bend and a man hailed them. "Help! We need help!"

Denys pulled up on the reins, slowing his horse as the man and a boy rushed up to them. "How may we be of assistance?"

The man pointed at a horse farther down the road, its owner lying on the ground. "He suffered a coughing fit. My son came and got me, but when we returned, he was passed out. He's barely breathing. I believe he may be one of yours."

Denys' eyes narrowed. "One of mine?"

"A nobleman, sir."

Denys dismounted as his men spread out to cover the area. He strode over to the prone man and took a knee, gasping at the sight of François, blood trickling from his mouth, his breathing shallow. "Lord François, are you all right?"

François' eyes fluttered open and he reached up. "Sir Denys, is that you?"

Denys pointed at Marshal Guillaume. "Collect the wagon at Thomas' residence and send a man on ahead to the Palace. Tell the doctor to be ready."

"Yes, sir!" Guillaume relayed the orders and his men sprang into action as Denys returned his attention to the ailing man.

"I have sinned, my friend."

Denys took François hand and squeezed it. "I know. I've known all along."

"But how could you?"

"God has a plan for all of us, and He made me a part of yours."

Guillaume handed Denys a flask and he held it up to François' lips. He drank eagerly, his Adam's apple bobbing, and he breathed a little easier.

"The baby. It's not ours."

"I know. What do you want to do?"

François closed his eyes for a moment. "I know

what I should do, but I can't. If I return him to his parents, then my daughters and wife are doomed."

Denys clasped the man's hand to his chest, shaking his head. "No, my friend. All is not lost. You know I said I was here to help. Well, let me help you now."

"How? How can you possibly help me? I am about to die, to burn in Hell for what I've done, tormented with the knowledge that I failed to save my family."

"Let *me* save your family, Lord François."

François stared up at him, confused. "I don't understand."

"My intention was to visit you tomorrow to ask permission to court your daughter, the beautiful Helene. With your permission, I intend to marry her. Though my title and wealth aren't as great as yours, I have more than enough to ensure the stability of your family. Your daughters will be welcomed into my home as sisters, your wife as the matriarch. They will all maintain their good name and reputation until they can be married to proper families, where they will be taken care of by their husbands, and provided the means to properly care for your wife. I swear this as a knight and as your friend, in front of the Lord and all these witnesses. Your family won't be left destitute. Let Helene save me from the wretched path I had laid out before me. Let her help me become a better man so I can save your family."

François squeezed Denys' hand, staring up at him. "I always knew you were a better man than the image you projected. You reminded me of myself when I was younger, a fool with wealth and title, but the love of a good woman turned me around. My Denise saved me from a reckless future that would have led me to dying alone, having left nothing behind. You have my permission to court my daughter, and should she choose to marry you, then you also have my blessing." Tears rolled from his eyes. "Thank you for allowing me to die in peace, but I have yet another favor to ask of you."

"Anything."

"Find the baby's family and return him, and make sure that Madeleine is safe."

"You have my word."

François closed his eyes and coughed, once again a fit developing. Denys rolled him onto his side as the carriage arrived. François' hand darted out, gripping Denys' tunic.

"Tell them not what I have done, but only that I loved them."

And with that, he gasped, collapsing into the mud, his chest still, the life fading from his eyes. Denys stepped back and made the sign of the cross then stood at attention, his guard surrounding him doing the same as he said a silent prayer for the soul of the man whose family he'd just promised to save.

Passe's chest heaved. His fists ached as he held them up in front of him. He could see the bloodied, cracked skin in the moonlight, and as he slowly turned, he let the muscles relax, the fingers slowly unfurling. Everyone was down except for him. Most were dead. Some lay bleeding out. Richart had been one of the last to die, hiding behind his men, but Bertaut had managed to get a blade through, piercing the man's heart before falling to the final two blades of Richart's combined forces. In their shock, Passe had advanced with his dagger in hand, sticking the blade between the ribs of one and, unable to remove it, using his fists on the other before twisting his neck and breaking it.

But it was over. He had won, though at what cost? All of his men were dead, as were Olivier's and Richart's. He could rule everything, but how? All that was left was an empire of dirt, of muddied streets, with no one who would respect him after what had happened. With no one to project the force he needed, he would have to rebuild from scratch, yet the void left behind by three major gangs being wiped out in one night would be quickly filled by people like Thibault who would take over his women, take over his loans, take over the stragglers that still remained.

He might have survived the night, but his life was over.

"Now it's my turn," said a voice from behind him. He turned to see a large Templar walking toward him, a sneer on his face. "I'll show you what we do to people who kidnap children."

Passe gulped and raised his weary fists. It appeared God wasn't finished punishing him tonight.

Gerart watched from an alleyway with his father as the Templar caught Passe's first punch, gripping one of the famed iron fists in mid-air before delivering a flurry of blows to Passe's face. The Templar let go then raised both fists over his head, dropping them down hard on Passe's head. The wretch collapsed to his knees and the fists raised up again, then slammed down once more. Passe tipped to his side, collapsing in the mud.

The Templar stood over him. "Do you have anything to say before you meet your maker?"

Passe spat. "Just get this over with."

"As you wish." The Templar raised a foot and slammed it down on Passe's head, the crunch of his skull echoing through the streets lined with onlookers who cheered the outcome.

"Well, I guess I'm not getting my thousand deniers," said Gerart with disappointment.

His father grabbed him by the nape of the neck and shook him gently, then held him tight against his side. "No, I suppose not."

"Can I still come home?"

His father laughed. "Of course you can. I'm not taking you back because of a thousand deniers. I'm taking you back because you're my son."

Gerart's eyes burned and his chest ached as he wrapped his arms around his father, the sobs finally unleashed. "I'm so sorry for what I did."

His father shook as he embraced him, his voice cracking repeatedly. "You have nothing to be sorry for. I'm the one who was at fault. Now, let's get home and see your mother and sisters."

Gerart eyed the street where the fight had taken place, those gathered slowly dispersing, the shutters on the windows closing and the Templars, on horseback, fading into the night, Passe and his men, and those they had fought, left in the streets to be dealt with in the morning.

Then a thought occurred to him. "Father, if you steal from a thief, is it still stealing?"

"Of course it is."

Gerart frowned. "Do you think a rich man would give a reward if something that had been stolen from him was returned?"

"Just what are you getting at?"

He jerked a thumb at the road behind them where the nobleman had just died. "I saw a fancy dagger hanging on Passe's wall. I think it might have belonged to the rich man. If Passe and everyone's dead, it's just going to disappear. If I get it, maybe we can return it."

His father smiled. "You might be on to something there, boy. You go get it and I'll tell the men to wait."

Gerart grinned and sprinted toward Passe's residence, happier than he had been for as long as he could remember. His father still loved him and had welcomed him back into his home, and if he could retrieve the dagger and return it to its rightful owner, the reward might well be worth his share of the thousand deniers promised him. He smiled up at the heavens, thanking the good Lord for saving his soul from the likes of a devil such as Passe.

De Rancourt Family Farm
Crécy-la-Chapelle, Kingdom of France

"Is anyone home?" yelled Marcus.

As the procession turned onto the property, Beatrice poked a head out an open window. "They're here! They're here!"

Tanya rushed past the group, bowling over Jacques and Pierre as she spun around in excitement, her heavy tail smacking the children. Lady Joanne emerged from the farmhouse, a smile of relief on her face. Everyone came to a halt in front of the door and dismounted as David and Jeremy collected the horses and headed for the stables.

Beatrice's eyes shot wide at the new arrivals. "Madeleine, is that you?"

Madeleine's jaw dropped as she raised her head, the poor woman's face still bandaged. "Beatrice? For the love of God, what are you doing here? We all thought you were dead!"

Beatrice laughed. "We almost were!"

Madeleine gasped, apparently recognizing Lady Joanne, and curtsied. "Milady, I was certain you were!"

Joanne smiled. "It's a long story. And how are your lord and lady?"

Madeleine's face clouded over and Marcus held out a hand. "It's a long and disturbing story that we'll share, however, for now, let's just say that Miss Madeleine and her niece and nephew will be staying with us."

"For how long?" asked Joanne.

"Indefinitely, if they desire."

Joanne's eyes flashed concern, but she offered a welcoming smile. "Then let's get you inside. You must be tired after your journey."

Thomas and Isabelle followed the rest inside, leaving Simon and Marcus alone. They had remained in Paris for several more days as inquiries were made to confirm that Madeleine and the children were indeed safe. Thibault had confirmed that the vast majority of Passe's, Richart's, and Olivier's men were dead, something she was delighted about, her business no doubt set to expand. She had made certain the word was spread that anyone dealing in children would feel the wrath of the Templars, though she doubted it would have any effect, nor did he. The money was simply too good, though perhaps it would make someone think twice. She had also made it known that the contract on Madeleine and the children was canceled.

Lord François had already been buried in the family graveyard on his estate, and his brother had arrived just yesterday with his own family, graciously giving François' wife and five daughters one month to vacate the property. But Denys was a man of his word and had vowed they could all live under his roof, and the wedding was already planned between him and Helene in the coming weeks so no scandal could occur within the Court. The baby had been returned to his family, a woman of ill repute once employed by Passe remembering where he had been taken from. Tragically, his parents had been murdered during the abduction, but his grandparents on both sides were eager to raise him.

So many had died, so many had suffered injuries that would haunt them for the rest of their days, all for title and wealth, all because women were little more than property to the King of France and in Christendom in general. He sighed, and Simon looked at him.

"What's on your mind?"

"I'm just happy I have nothing but my title left."

"Don't forget this land."

Marcus' eyes narrowed. "Technically, I suppose, I don't own this land. It actually belongs to young Jacques, who would have inherited it from his father."

"So, he's my lord and not you?"

Marcus chuckled. "Would you prefer one who will order you to shovel out the barn and has no muscles to help, or one who will shovel by your side?"

Simon turned up his nose as he glanced back at the barn. "Do you think David and Jeremy had enough time to take care of that little problem before they left?"

Marcus smiled and slapped his friend on the shoulder. "I don't know. How about we go find out?"

Simon groaned. "I haven't been home five minutes and you already have me shoveling shit?"

Marcus tossed his head back, roaring with laughter. "Yes, but at least we're home."

And as they walked up the hill toward their barracks, he smiled at the sounds of their growing family in the farmhouse, and stared over at the small graveyard where his sister and her husband rested, thanking her for giving him the life he had never dreamed he wanted.

THE END

ACKNOWLEDGMENTS

I love writing this series. One of the many reasons is that it is a complete escape from modern-day problems. With the pandemic in full swing as of this writing, escape is more important now than ever, both for the reader and the writer.

For me, writing this was a pleasure. No viruses, no masks, no vaccines, no social distancing. As well, no Internet, no social media, no modern-day problems.

Just simple problems of the past. Bad guys to bag, shit to shovel.

When we were stationed in West Germany, we lived near pig farms where at various points of the year, they would spread the manure on the fields. The stench was unbelievable, and now that I think of it, perhaps modern-day problems aren't so bad.

This novel does pose an interesting question that in the civilized world we don't face, and that is the right of inheritance being restricted to men. Writing this had me wondering how far I would go if faced with a situation similar to Lord François'. Fortunately, despite my only child being a daughter, I will never have to deal with that injustice, though I do know I wouldn't kidnap a newborn.

I'd kill my brother.

Just kidding.

As usual, there are people to thank. My dad, as always, for the research, Deborah Wilson for some equine info, and of course, my wife, daughter, my late mother who will always be an angel on my shoulder as

I write, as well as my friends for their continued support, and my fantastic proofreading team!

To those who have not already done so, please visit my website at www.jrobertkennedy.com, then sign up for the Insider's Club to be notified of new book releases. Your email address will never be shared or sold.

Thank you once again for reading.

CPSIA information can be obtained
at www.ICGtesting.com
Printed in the USA
LVHW101418120222
710995LV00004B/165